WHERE'S AUDREY?

A. L. JAMBOR

Woofie

ISBN:978-099036367

Cover Design by Design by Amy Jambor

Photo Credits

© Can Stock Photo / dvarg

© Can Stock Photo/ Tawng

This book is dedicated to my mother, Grace. She passed on her love of reading to me.

Acknowledgments

I want to acknowledge the contribution of my friend and editor, Loraine O'Connell. Loraine's suggestions and knowledge have helped shape my books for three years. Her assistance is priceless.

Chapter One

MEL JONES TAPPED THE KEYS ON THE KEYBOARD SEARCHING for a flight to Tampa. Every flight had a layover in Atlanta.

Shit, she thought. Six hours to fly from New Jersey to Florida. She hadn't planned on taking her vacation there, but her great-grandmother had called and asked her to and Mel didn't have the heart to refuse her, especially when Nana Grace offered to pay her airfare.

"I haven't heard from Audrey in weeks," Grace said. Audrey was Mel's great-great-aunt.

"Where does she live?" Mel asked

"In Largo. It won't take long, dear. All you have to do is go to the trailer and see if she's all right."

Mel didn't know her aunt. She had only met her once, when she was six. She wondered how Audrey would feel if she just showed up on her doorstep. "Did you call the police?"

"They won't do anything until she's missing for two days, and I don't know for sure that she is missing."

Mel wanted to protest again, but something in Grace's

voice stopped her. She was genuinely concerned about her sister, and Mel was her only family.

Well, that wasn't exactly true. But Mel's mother, Linda, was out on the West Coast and Mel's grandmother, Grace's daughter, Laura, was on crutches. Besides, Mel had taken her two weeks of vacation and her best friend, Lisa, was using her dad's time share condo on Clearwater Beach. She had invited Mel to join her, but at the time, Mel couldn't afford a plane ticket. Now, she could cruise by Audrey's trailer and then head on over to Clearwater Beach.

"You can stay with my friend, Vera," Grace said. "She lives in a park down the road from Audrey's."

"Why hasn't she checked on Audrey?" Mel asked, seeing a chance to opt out.

"They haven't spoken in years. I can't ask Vera to check on her."

Mel rolled her eyes. "Okay. I'll go."

Now, as she looked at the flights, she thought about driving to Florida. She would save money on a car rental and…no. She couldn't drive straight through alone. So she began scrolling through the flights again.

Spirit left from Atlantic City and offered nonstop flights. She'd get to Tampa in two hours; she could visit Aunt Audrey and spend, say, an hour or so, then go to Clearwater Beach. It would work.

Mel lived alone. She had since she graduated from Brookdale Community College with a two-year degree. She still didn't know what she wanted to be, but working as a manager in Starbucks suited her for now. It paid better than most retail jobs, and Mel was a morning person, which meant she didn't mind getting up at five a.m. every morning.

Getting two weeks off at Christmas was unheard of in retail, but Mel hadn't taken a vacation in three years. Someone at corporate noticed and told her supervisor she'd have to take two weeks off. If there was no one else available, he'd just have to cover her hours.

Mel wasn't thrilled with the idea of taking time off since she couldn't afford to actually go anywhere, but now she was grateful she'd pushed herself so hard. Two weeks in Florida was just what she needed.

She went to her closet and looked at her clothes. Everything in it was for work. She didn't have normal clothes anymore. Her shoes, too, were for work. Mel sighed. She'd have to buy something to wear. At least a bathing suit. She went back to her computer and began searching for clothes in brick and mortar stores.

Mel's body was one of those hard to fit bodies that drive women crazy. The waist on this pair of pants fit, but her ass wouldn't fill the seat. Finding a pair of pants that fit right was nearly impossible without having someone take them in at the crotch. Grandma Laura was good at that, but since her accident, she'd been taking it easy and Mel didn't want to ask her to do a rush job. She'd have to look for dresses or skirts.

She found two cute dresses at Forever 21 and checked availability at the mall. They had her size! She grabbed her purse. She looked in her wallet. Both her credit cards were maxed out and her checking account held her two weeks' vacation money. That was for bills. Shit. Now what would she do? Just as she was contemplating calling the whole thing off, her phone rang. It was Nana Grace.

"What will you need for the trip?" she asked.

"The ticket will be kind of expensive because I'm making it at the last minute."

"I'm going to give you two thousand dollars. Will that be enough?"

Mel began to salivate. She could get the dresses and maybe a pair of cute shoes. "More than enough. Are you sure you can afford that?"

"Yes, dear. Did you find a flight?"

"Yup. I just have to book it."

"Well, come and get the money so you can put it into your bank."

"Thanks, Nana. I'll be right over."

Two thousand dollars. Mel wondered if she'd ever be able to give her future granddaughter that kind of money without a second thought. Not working at Starbucks she wouldn't. She decided to use this time off to rethink her career choice and figure out what she wanted to do with the rest of her life.

Nana Grace let Mel into her apartment. The year before, Laura had helped Grace move into the senior complex she herself occupied. They lived on the same floor. Grace was spry and had been helping her injured daughter recover from a car accident that had left Laura with a broken leg. She cooked for Laura and made sure her clothes were clean.

"Hello, dear," Grace said.

"Hey, Nana," Mel said. She gave Grace a hug. "You look tired."

"I'm all right. I just got done doing laundry is all. I have a check for you here."

Grace went to her small roll-top desk and got the check. She brought it to Mel. When Mel took it, Grace held her hand.

"I do appreciate you doing this."

"It's no problem, Nana."

"I've very worried about Aud. I tried calling and writing, but she hasn't responded."

"Doesn't she have a neighbor you could call?"

"I'm ashamed to say I don't know them. And when I call the park office, it rings and rings. No one answers."

"That's weird."

"Indeed. So, do you have clothes to take with you?"

Nana had helped Laura raise Mel. She was always concerned about what Mel wore.

"I'm going to the mall to buy a couple of dresses."

"I can take in your pants if you buy them."

"No. It's Florida. It's warm. I'll be fine."

"Okay." Nana leaned over and hugged Mel. "Call me as soon as you get there. I want to know everything that happens."

"I will," Mel said. "I'm gonna check on Grandma while I'm here."

"I'll go with you. I have to take her clean clothes over there."

Mel carried the basket and followed Grace. Grace used a four-wheeled walker with a shelf for sitting or carrying things. She moved quicker than Mel expected. Laura was three doors down and when they got to her door, Grace opened it without knocking.

Laura was in her recliner with her legs up. She smiled when she saw Mel and put out her hands. Mel put the basket down and went to her to accept a big hug.

"I hear you're going to Florida," Laura said.

"Yeah. Nana's sending me."

"I'm worried about Aud, too. She didn't send me a birthday card. It isn't like her to forget."

"How long has it been since you guys heard from her?" Mel asked.

Nana put her finger on her cheek while she thought. "I talked to her in September."

"That was what, three months ago?" Mel asked. "Why have you waited so long to find out what happened to her?"

"Well, I had the accident, and Nana was in the hospital in October."

"But still, no one called during all that time?"

"We've been busy," Laura said. "You get busy, don't you?"

"Why all the sudden do you want me to go look for her?"

Nana sat on the sofa near Laura's recliner. She looked embarrassed. "I had a dream about her."

"Mom thinks she's in trouble."

"Oh. Okay. So you had a dream," Mel said to Grace.

"Don't pick on her," Laura said. "It was a terrible dream."

"She was hurt. I couldn't get to her."

Nana Grace looked dejected. Mel bit her lower lip. She went to the sofa and sat next to Grace.

"I'll need her address and her phone number," Mel said.

"Go to my desk and get my address book," Laura said.

Mel got up and went to the desk. Laura was a neat person, and the address book was perfectly aligned next to the faux leather blotter.

"Bring paper and a pen, too."

The pens were in a faux leather cup that matched the blotter, and there were Post-its in a cube. Mel took a pen and one Post-it back to Laura.

Mel envied Laura's penmanship. She had graceful, female handwriting, while Mel's resembled a doctor's scrawl. When Laura was done, Audrey's name and address looked like the script on a wedding invitation.

"Do you have a picture of Audrey, Laura?" Grace asked.

"I think there's one in that photo album in the bookcase."

Laura pointed and Mel looked to where she was pointing. A small bookcase sat against the wall between the living room and the kitchen. She went to it and pulled out the large photo album, then brought it to Laura.

"It's in here somewhere," Laura said, flipping through the pages. "Here."

She pulled it out of the black corner holders and handed it to Mel. Audrey was leaning against a tree.

"That was when she first moved down there," Laura said.

"Let me see it," Grace said. Mel handed it to her. "Oh, yes. I think she sent me that one too."

"Do you have one that's more recent?" Mel asked. "That was what, twenty years ago?"

"That's the only one I have. She didn't send any after that."

"Didn't you ever go and visit her?" Mel asked.

"I wanted to go," Grace said. "But I just couldn't find the right time."

"In twenty years, you couldn't find the right time?" Mel said.

"It's harder to travel when you get older," Laura said.

"But you weren't that old," Mel said.

"I have a job," Laura said.

"Okay," Mel said. "So, I guess I'll be going. I have stuff to do."

"Call me as soon as you get there," Laura said.

"I'll call you both."

After bidding them both goodbye, Mel headed to Grace's bank. She cashed the check, then deposited the cash into her own checking account. She went to the mall, bought the cute dresses, found a pair of shoes in Payless, and went home.

Chapter Two

THE FLIGHT TO TAMPA WAS UNEVENTFUL. MEL WORE ONE
of her new dresses and the shoes she'd bought. She had
checked her suitcase and breathed a sigh of relief when it
appeared on the carousel. The rental car was also waiting
for Mel when she arrived. So far, so good.

The GPS on her iPhone led her directly to Audrey's
mobile home park. As Mel turned into the park, she
noticed how nice it looked. She had imagined one of those
broken down parks where large pit bulls guarded rusted-
out single-wides with old swing sets in the front yard. This
was nothing like that.

Large palm trees and ancient oak trees lined the road.
Each house had its own generous lot, and they were all
pruned and plucked to perfection. Everyone she passed
waved at her, and she felt compelled to wave back.

The homes were decorated with strings of lights,
blown-up snowmen in bubbles with snow blowing all
around, and lots of candy canes. The festive atmosphere
was depressing. It served to remind Mel that Christmas was
coming and nothing could stop it.

Audrey lived at 298. Her road was a cul-de-sac. Her home was the second one in. Mel parked in front. She noticed an old Mercury sitting in Audrey's driveway and saw her last name on the mailbox, "Glenn." She got out of her car and grabbed her purse. She threw it over her shoulder and walked to the door leading into the porch.

The home had a screened porch and a carport. There were no decorations adorning Audrey's home. Either she, like Mel, didn't feel the need to cover her abode in tinsel, or, at her age, it was just too hard to hang the lights from the carport roof.

Mel rang the bell next to the screen door and heard footsteps approaching. They were fast and heavy, unlike those of an elderly woman. She heard the sliding glass door open and a man stuck his head out.

He was gorgeous, and Mel felt her cheeks grow hot. His blue eyes under black lashes were mesmerizing, and his black hair fell in soft layers as if he hadn't had a haircut in a while. It suited him. He looked surprised when he saw her, then caught himself and smiled.

"Yes?" he said.

"Hi," Mel replied. "I'm looking for my aunt."

"Um, you sure you have the right house?"

"Her name is on the mailbox and that's her car." She had no idea if it was Audrey's car or not, but Mel pointed to the huge Mercury parked in the carport, thinking that would add weight to her assumption that this was her aunt's house.

He came to the screen door. He was wearing some sort of cologne and the scent wafted through the holes in the screen. Mel liked it. She also liked his white, even teeth.

"What's your aunt's name?"

"Audrey Glenn."

"Audrey never mentioned having a niece. Well, not one your age," he said. He smiled.

"My grandmother asked me to stop by. Audrey's her sister. She hasn't heard from her in a while and is worried."

"Your grandmother, huh? You got some ID?"

"What are you, a cop?" Mel said.

"Naw. I promised Audrey I'd look after the place. I'm just being careful."

Mel reached into her purse and took out her Jersey license. She held it up.

"That doesn't help much. You have a different last name," he said, but he unhooked the lock and let her in.

She hesitated while he held the screen door open. What if this guy had hurt Audrey? What if he killed Mel and cut up her body? The other homes were close by. She could scream and someone would hear her. She shook the thoughts out of her head and followed him inside.

The home was a double-wide. The porch led into a long living room. Next to that was a dining room, and the kitchen was off the dining room. Mel assumed the bedrooms and bath were in the back.

She looked at the pictures on the built-in shelves and saw her high school graduation picture.

"You knew who I was," she said.

He glanced at the photo. "I know. I just wanted to see what you'd do."

Very funny, she thought. "So, where's Audrey?"

"She went on one of those holiday cruises. She won't be back until after New Year's."

"Is there any way to get in touch with her?"

"She's out at sea. I don't think you can call her there."

Mel didn't believe there was no way to get a message to her aunt.

"What cruise?"

"She's going to Europe."

"Europe? Did she go alone?"

"She went with a friend."

"What's the friend's name?"

Mel wasn't backing down. Something about this didn't feel right, and she was getting frustrated with his answers.

"Ginny," he said. "She's a widow who lives in another park."

How convenient, Mel thought. She looked around the room. There was a built-in desk in the inner wall that divided the living room from the kitchen. She walked over to it and began pulling out drawers.

"I don't think you should be doing that," he said.

"What's your name?" Mel asked.

"Jason. That's Audrey's stuff."

"I'm sure she wouldn't mind me looking in here."

He walked over and gently pushed her away.

"I'm responsible for her stuff. I think she would mind."

His voice wasn't as friendly as it had been. Mel didn't like the way he'd touched her. And this time, she noticed his eyes were bloodshot.

"Fine," she said. She wrote down her phone number. "If she gets in touch with you, give her my number."

"Sure. No problem."

She took one last look around. The place hadn't been vacuumed in a while and there was dust everywhere. Dishes were on the dining table, a lot of dishes, like it had been months since they were taken to the kitchen and washed. If Audrey had gone on a holiday cruise, she would have left a few days ago. Mel doubted she would have left her house in such disarray.

She let herself out the screen door and got into the car. She sat there for a few minutes trying to collect her thoughts. Something was wrong. Jason might have been good-looking, but there was something about him that bothered her. For one thing, he was too young. She didn't think Audrey would entrust her home to anyone under fifty. And he looked like he was on something.

She dialed Laura's number. Laura answered and Mel told her about Jason. Laura felt as Mel had – that Audrey wouldn't have someone so young housesitting while she went on a cruise. And she would never leave her house looking like that.

"She wouldn't have gone on a cruise without telling Mom," Laura said. "Especially overseas."

"Why especially overseas?" Mel asked.

"I don't think she had a passport."

"She could have gotten one."

"Not unless she fixed the glitch."

The glitch? "What glitch?" Mel asked.

"The glitch that prevented her from getting a passport the first time she applied for one."

"What glitch?"

"She and Mom were born in Cuba on Guantanamo Bay. Their birth certificates were wrong, and they had to go through so much rigmarole to change them that Audrey just gave up."

"When was this?" Mel asked.

"Oh, about twenty years ago."

So, Audrey couldn't get a passport twenty years ago. Maybe she'd had the glitch fixed. Maybe she was able to get a passport. Maybe Jason was a lying scumbag.

Chapter Three

MEL SAT IN FRONT OF AUDREY'S HOUSE FOR A WHILE. SHE looked at the homes on each side of Audrey's, then she looked across the street. There was an old woman sitting on the porch of the one directly across from Audrey's. The Shih Tzu with her kept barking.

"Shut up, Maurice!" the woman cried over and over.

Mel heard a knock on the passenger window and jumped. She turned and saw an old man. She turned the key in the ignition and lowered the window.

"I saw you go to the house," he said. "Are you looking for Audrey?"

"Yes, I am. "

He looked toward Audrey's home and then back at Mel. "I haven't seen her in a long time."

"How long is a long time?"

"Months. She used to come to the pool. Some of us were getting worried."

"Did you talk to the police?"

"They won't do anything."

"How do you know if you didn't report her missing?"

"We didn't know if she was missing or not. We thought maybe she was sick and he," the man pointed at Audrey's with his thumb, "was taking care of her."

"Did you knock on the door and ask him about her?"

The man looked down at the ground. "He's kind of young. I don't want any trouble. I have to live here."

"Then why...oh, never mind."

"I just thought I should tell you."

"Well, thanks," she said out loud and "for nothing" under her breath. He backed away and she closed the window. She hadn't remembered to ask his name and he hadn't offered it.

Mel looked at the woman across the street. She didn't look too friendly. She contemplated talking to her, but her stomach rumbled. She was hungry. She wanted to go to Clearwater Beach and stay with Lisa but felt obligated to find out what happened to Audrey first. She'd have to start looking for a hotel room.

Mel started the car and did a K-turn. The old guy had mentioned there was a pool in the park. Grace had said there was an office, too. Mel could speak to the manager.

"You're gonna have to wait," she told her stomach as she turned onto the main road and began looking for the pool. She found it. It was in the center of the park.

The office was a nondescript, cement block building painted white. It sat directly in front of the pool. She parked the car out front and looked for the entrance. When she got inside, she saw an elderly woman sitting behind a gray metal desk.

"Hello," she said.

"Hi. My name is Mel Jones. I'm looking for Audrey Glenn. She's my aunt."

"I know Audrey."

"We haven't heard from her in a while and we're starting to worry about her."

The woman pursed her lips. "You know? I haven't seen her in a while."

"Does anyone check on them, the residents, if they don't show up for a while?"

"There's no system in place if that's what you mean, but neighbors tend to notice if someone hasn't been seen for a while."

Mel saw a brochure on the desk touting the joys of living in an over fifty-five community. "Aren't there rules about how old you have to be to live here?"

"Yes. You have to be over fifty-five. Sometimes we relax the rules if someone is married to a younger person, but otherwise, it's fifty-five."

"There's a guy living in her house. He's definitely not over fifty-five. He said he's staying there while she's on a cruise."

"Well, that seems odd. I'll have to ask the manager if she knows about this."

"Has Audrey been paying her rent on time?" Mel asked.

The woman opened a drawer and pulled out a blue ledger. She turned the pages and found Audrey's name.

"She's paid her rent on time every month."

"Does she come in and pay it?"

"No. She leaves an envelope with a money order in the drop-box."

Mel pulled a small wire bound notebook out of her purse."

"Can you lend me a pen?" she asked, and the woman handed her a blue Bic. "What's your name?"

"Peggy. Peggy March. I work here three days a week."

"Thanks, Ms. March." Mel wrote down her name, and

then she wrote her own phone number down on a separate page and tore it out of the notebook. "Can you give this to the manager?" She handed Peggy the piece of paper and the Bic pen. "It's my phone number."

"Certainly," Peggy said. "The manager's name is Nancy. She's out showing a unit to a nice couple from Minnesota."

"But she's usually here during the day?"

"Oh, yes."

"If you hear anything, or if she knows anything about Audrey, please call me."

She left the office and sighed. The weather was gorgeous, but she hardly noticed it. She was worried about Audrey.

The last and only time she had seen her aunt was just before Audrey moved to Florida. Nana Grace had thrown her a going away party, and six-year-old Mel had sung a song. She could barely remember what Audrey looked like, but she remembered how soft her cheeks were, and that she smelled of Chanel No. 5.

Mel looked at the old people riding by on three-wheel bicycles or in golf carts. She rarely saw people this old, except for Nana Grace, and looking at them now, it was easy to see why they would be afraid of a guy like Jason. Still, you would think that one of them would have asked the police to check on her. She looked at the pool behind the office and decided to walk over and see if anyone there knew Audrey.

The pool was surrounded by lounge chairs. It was two in the afternoon. It was hot, and the sun could be brutal. The chairs were empty.

"Damn," Mel said. She'd have to come back later.

She left the park and drove down Ulmerton Road, one of the main thoroughfares running through Largo. Mel was frustrated. Where was Audrey? Mel didn't buy Jason's story that she went to Europe on a cruise. The Caribbean maybe, but Europe? Audrey would have told someone. She would have told Grace.

Mel wondered how Jason came to be in Audrey's home. How long had he been living there? Why wasn't he working during the day?

She was driving aimlessly and came to a traffic light. To her left, she saw a sign for the Pinellas County Sheriff's Office. She went up the road a bit and made a U-turn to get there. She parked the car and went to the visitor's entrance.

It was a big office. There were several windows in the reception area, and behind each, a large black woman. It was as if they'd been cloned. Mel sat and waited until one of them looked her way.

"Hi," Mel said.

"Can I help you?" the woman asked. She wore a badge that read "Sophie."

"My name is Mel Jones and I was wondering where I could file a missing persons report?"

"How long has the person been missing?"

"That's just it. I'm not sure."

"We can't file a report until the person has been missing forty-eight hours."

"This is my elderly aunt. She lives in a mobile home. She hasn't called her sister in a long time and there's some young guy living in her home."

"Has he reported her missing?"

"No. But don't you think it's weird he'd be there alone?"

"Did you ask him where she was?"

"Yes. He said she went on a cruise, but she would have told her sister she was leaving the country. She's ninety!"

Sophie pursed her lips. "Like I said, we can't file a report until they've been gone two days. She's old, though. Wait here a minute."

Sophie got up. Mel watched her walk toward the back of the office where some deputies sat at desks. Sophie stopped and talked to a young deputy, a man with short dark blond hair. He was nice-looking, and for the second time that day, Mel felt her cheeks grow hot. Mel hadn't been on a date in a long time. The idea of opening an account on Match.com entered her mind. It wasn't the first time.

Cut it out, she thought. Focus on Audrey.

Sophie returned and sat down. "Deputy O'Keefe will help you. He'll be out in a minute."

"Thank you," Mel said. She smiled broadly, but Sophie was looking at her computer monitor.

Deputy O'Keefe came through the side door. Mel notice he had blue eyes. He was tall, very tall, and she imagined he had a great chest under his uniform.

"Are you Mel Jones?" he asked.

"Yes," she said.

"I'm Deputy O'Keefe. You have some questions regarding your aunt?"

Mel walked over to him.

"I went to see her this afternoon and I found some guy living in her mobile home. He said she went on a cruise, but she never told my grandmother she was going."

"And you think something happened to her?"

"I don't know. I just think it's weird he's living there and she's gone without a word to anyone."

"Why is it weird he's living there?"

"Because he's too young. He can't be older than thirty."

"We can take a ride over there if you'd like."

Mel hadn't expected this. "That would be great."

He led Mel to an unmarked patrol car and she got into the passenger side. There was a computer in the center attached to an adjustable arm. When Deputy O'Keefe got in, he punched something into the computer, then started the car.

"Has your aunt ever gone off without telling anyone before?"

"I don't think so. I don't know her very well. She's my great-great aunt." She glanced sideways at his face. "I just didn't like the guy. Audrey never told my grandmother she had someone living with her."

"When was the last time anyone talked to her?"

"The guy living next to her said he hasn't seen her in months."

"I mean relatives, like your grandmother."

"She hasn't heard in a while, but I don't know exactly how long it's been."

"Which park does she live in?"

Mel pulled out her phone and pulled up the GPS. "Holiday Oaks."

"That's just down the road."

There was traffic on Ulmerton Road. Deputy O'Keefe kept his eyes on the road. He didn't ask any more questions.

Mel remembered Nana Grace saying she had talked to Audrey in September. She felt embarrassed. Someone from the family should have come down and checked on her a long time ago.

Mel thought of her mother, Linda. She was a hairdresser for some TV show in California. She could go all over the world, but she couldn't check on her elderly aunt. That was typical of her mother. Always putting herself first and the hell with everybody else.

"What the number of her unit?" the deputy asked.

"298," Mel said.

They parked in front of Audrey's home. The Mercury was still in the driveway.

"Come with me," Deputy O'Keefe said.

She got out and followed him to the porch. He rang the bell and in a few minutes, Jason appeared from behind the sliding glass door.

"Yes," he said.

"Can you come to the door, sir?" Deputy O'Keefe asked.

Jason came to the screen door.

"Could you step outside?"

Jason stepped outside. He glared at Mel and the look made her cringe.

"Ms. Jones came to the sheriff's office because she's concerned about her aunt. She says you told her that her aunt was on a cruise."

"Yeah. She left a few days ago."

Deputy O'Keefe took his notebook out. "What cruise line would that be?"

Without missing a beat, Jason said, "Disney."

"Disney goes to Europe?" Mel asked.

"Sure it does," Jason said, but his cheeks were turning red.

"Sir, how are you related to the owner of this home?"

"I'm a friend. I've got permission to be here."

"Do you have something written that says you have a legal right to be on the premises?"

"Yeah. Audrey gave me a letter. Wait here and I'll get it."

"May I enter the home?" Deputy O'Keefe asked.

"Uh, sure," Jason said.

"I'll go with you," Deputy O'Keefe said, but he signaled Mel to wait outside.

They came back a few minutes later and Deputy O'Keefe showed Mel a letter saying Jason had permission to be in Audrey's house in her absence. It was signed by Audrey, but Mel wasn't sure if it was her aunt's signature or not. She tried to remember the birthday cards Audrey had sent her, but they were usually signed Aunt Audrey, and she hadn't had one in a while.

Deputy O'Keefe handed the letter back to Jason and gave him his business card.

"Please have Ms. Glenn contact me when she returns."

"I will, Deputy," Jason said. He looked smug and Mel was fuming.

"That's it?" she said as she and Deputy O'Keefe walked back to the cruiser.

"He had a letter."

"But he could have written it himself."

"Unless you have proof that something has happened to your aunt, there's nothing else I can do. You can file a missing persons report when we get back to the station, but we won't be able to follow up on it until after the new year."

"Why not?"

"Because he says she's on a cruise. Do you know differently?"

"No."

"Then this is how it has to be. My name is Conner, by the way."

Mel was thinking about Audrey. "What?"

"Conner. It's my name." He smiled at her. "Where are you staying?"

"I don't know. I was going to stay with a friend, but I

was thinking of getting a hotel room here. I hate to go somewhere till I know what happened."

They drove back to the sheriff's office. When they got out of the car, he handed her his card. "That's got my cell on it. Call me when you know where you'll be."

She took the card. "You want my number?"

"Sure." She gave it to him and he noted it in his notebook.

"Do you want to file a report?" he asked.

She nodded and followed him into the station. He took her to his desk and filled out a report with the facts as she knew them. When they were done, he looked at her.

"I'm off at six," he said. "Do you want to get some dinner?"

Mel was floored. "Are you asking me out?"

He nodded. "You have to eat, right?"

"Yeah, but, my aunt is missing."

"I know. I guess it's a little inappropriate."

"Do ya think?"

He smiled. "Sorry. It's just that you're cute and I know you're just here for a short time."

She blushed. "I guess I do have to eat."

"Call me when you're settled. Like I said, I'm here till six and by the time I get home and change, it will be more like seven."

"Okay."

He walked her to the reception area and left her at the door. As she walked to her car, she thought she saw her aunt's Mercury parked at the back of the parking lot. It was too far away to tell, and the town was full of Mercurys. Old people loved the boxy cars.

She turned on the car and drove to the exit. The car she had seen was gone.

Chapter Four

Deputy Conner O'Keefe typed "Audrey Glenn" into the search box. Nothing came up. She'd never been arrested, nor had a traffic ticket. Then he typed in her address and got a hit. It was a call made to the sheriff's office three months before.

Someone had called the sheriff's office to report that something suspicious was going on at the mobile home. The sheriff received several calls a month from people who believed their neighbors were aliens, or someone they saw on a wanted poster in the post office. A deputy would follow up on some, while others were simply filed away. This one had been filed away.

Conner pulled up the transcript of the 911 call. The person calling was a man named Richard Norman and he lived in 300 – the home next to Audrey's. He told the dispatcher that something had happened to the lady living at 298 and he wanted someone to come out and investigate. When asked why he believed something had happened to her, he stated that a young man was living in her house and she hadn't been seen at the pool in over a month. No one was dispatched. No reason was noted.

Now, as Conner looked at the call, he thought about Jason. He took out his notebook. While he was in the home with him, Conner had asked Jason some questions. Jason's last name was Frye. Conner did a "Who's in Jail" search and found Jason's mug shot. He'd been arrested five years ago on a possession of cocaine charge. Nothing since. His case had been dismissed. There was another Jason Frye in the database, an older man. They could be related.

Jason had been cooperative when Conner questioned him. He showed Conner a letter with Audrey's signature stating he had her permission to stay in the house. At first, Conner didn't think much of it. A young person living in an over fifty-five park wasn't that unusual, but they were usually related to the owner. To have a stranger live there, though, would require permission from the park.

Conner knew he couldn't waste much time on the case. He'd have to wait the requisite forty-eight hours after the filing of the report to investigate. But he could patrol the neighborhood when he was out on his rounds.

———

MEL WAS AGGRAVATED. SHE WANTED TO FIND A HOTEL room, and they were all booked with holiday travelers. She also wanted to go to Lisa's condo, but she still didn't know what had happened to Audrey, and once she was with Lisa, she knew she wouldn't want to leave her.

Underneath it all, she was worried about Audrey. Her family was small. Her nana had been good to her and had asked for little in return. Her mother, Linda, had never been attentive toward her, but her grandmother, Laura, had raised her and always made her feel loved and wanted.

They were counting on her to find out what happened to Audrey.

Thinking of Linda made Mel angry. Her mother was a healthy woman in her forties, but her selfishness was legendary in the family. They all knew they couldn't depend on Linda to help out. She made her own plans and led her own life. She had abandoned Mel soon after she was born, leaving her with Laura. Once Linda had a steady job and a place to live, Laura insisted she spend the summer with her young daughter, and for reasons known only to Linda, she obeyed.

As soon as Mel graduated high school, however, Linda no longer felt an obligation to see Mel. She sent money to Laura for Mel's education, something that Laura had also insisted upon, and occasionally called Mel on her birthday, but that was the extent of her maternal obligation.

If she allowed herself to think about Linda too long, Mel would never get anything done. She would just stay angry. She banished the thought of her mother and again focused on Audrey.

Mel had parked the car in a McDonald's parking lot. She looked at the Christmas stickers on the eatery's windows. She had forgotten Christmas. She was in Florida. It was too warm for Christmas.

Growing up, Mel had longed to have the Christmases she saw other kids having, or saw in TV specials shown during that time of year. Laura was a wonderful substitute mother, and would try to replicate the old-fashioned holidays for Mel, but Mel always felt something was missing. She would often wonder where her father was and never got a straight answer regarding him.

Men were scarce in the Jones family. None of the women in her family had stayed married for long, and her mother hadn't been married at all. Even Nana Grace had divorced her husband. It was quite a scandal back in the day and had caused a breach between her and Audrey.

Women just didn't do that in their day, and Audrey was embarrassed by her sister's brazen disregard for the humiliation her actions brought on the family. In time, the sisters made up, but not without sacrifices on Grace's part. She had to admit her guilt, even though she felt totally justified in leaving her husband. It was the only way to mend the breach. Grace missed her sister, and this was the price she had to pay to have her back.

Mel opened her purse and took out the photo of Audrey. It had been taken in the 1990's. Mel smiled at the photo. Audrey looked happy. She was a pretty woman who had aged gracefully, but she didn't look like the type to take on a young lover, if that's what Jason had been to her. If her past actions showed anything about her, she would have been too concerned with appearances to live with him if they were indeed lovers.

What is Jason to you? Mel thought.

Mel shook her head. She didn't want to think of her aged aunt in flagrante delicto. She put the picture back in her purse. She was wondering where she would spend the night when her phone rang. It was Nana Grace.

"Hey, Nana."

"Hello, dear. I'm just calling to see that you got there all right."

"I did, and I'm sorry I forgot to call."

"It's fine. Were you able to see Audrey?"

Mel didn't want to tell her the truth, not until she knew what had happened to Audrey.

"Not yet. There was no one home when I stopped by."

"Oh, dear. Was her car there?"

"No. I guess she was out."

Well, if her car was gone, then it may be a good thing. It means she's able to drive."

"Yeah. I'm gonna try again tomorrow. I'm just trying to find a room for the night, and everything is booked."

"I talked to my friend, Vera. She said you could stay with her."

Mel cringed. She didn't want to stay at some old lady's house. It wasn't the way she'd envisioned her trip to sunny Florida.

"I don't know, Nana."

"She's a very nice person."

"I'm sure she is, but…"

"Mel, stop worrying about what she'll be like and go there. You need a roof over your head. All you have to do is smile and eat what she offers you. And it's free!"

"I know, Nana. I guess it's okay."

Grace gave her the address and Vera's phone number. When she hung up, Mel held the phone for a while before making the call. The sun was going down fast and if she didn't get moving, it would be harder to find Vera's home in the dark.

She dialed Vera's number and it was answered in two rings. Vera must have had the phone right next to her.

"Hello," she said.

"Hi, Vera. This is Mel, Grace's granddaughter."

"Oh, yes. She said you might be calling."

Mel closed her eyes. "She told me to call if I needed a place to stay."

"Certainly. Come on over."

Vera gave Mel directions to her house and Mel started the car. As she drove to Vera's mobile home park, she sighed.

EARLIER THAT AFTERNOON, CONNER DROVE THROUGH Holiday Oaks. He went by Audrey's home and saw an old man going to the mailbox next to hers. He stopped and got out of his cruiser.

"Sir," he said. The old man didn't turn. He didn't have his hearing aid in and never heard the car pulling up behind him. "Sir."

As Conner drew near, the old man sensed his presence and turned. He jumped.

"Dear Lord, you scared me."

"Sorry about that. I just wanted to ask you something about the lady who lives in that home."

Conner pointed to Audrey's home.

"Did that girl tell you what I told her?" the old man asked.

"No, but she did file a report. When was the last time you saw Audrey Glenn?"

"Months ago. She used to get her mail. She went to the pool, too."

Conner took out his notebook. "What's your name?"

"Why do you need my name?"

"I just like to keep notes of who I talk to."

"Richard. Richard Norman. But people here call me Dick."

Conner wrote it down. He also noted the man's mailbox number – 300. "Anything else you remember?"

"Just that I don't like that kid living there."

"Has he threatened you?"

"No. Why would he do that?" Dick's eyes were wide.

"No reason. I just thought since you said you didn't like him living there."

"Well, I don't. He doesn't belong here." Dick came closer to Conner. "I think he did something to her."

"Can you be more specific?"

"No. It's just a feeling."

"Did you ever see him touch her?"

"No. Nothing like that. I just don't like him is all."

"Has anyone else talked to you about Ms. Glenn?"

"Marge has. She lives over there." Dick pointed to the home across the street where Mel had seen the woman sitting on the porch earlier that day. "She sits out there all day. If anyone would see something, she would."

Conner wrote down her name. "Does she have a last name?"

"Winthrop."

"Mr. Norman, if you notice anything else, give me a call."

Conner handed Dick his card.

"Will do."

Conner got back into the cruiser and took off as Dick looked over at Audrey's home. He'd be happy to keep an eye on it and report what he saw to Deputy O'Keefe.

Chapter Five

VERA'S PARK WAS SMALLER THAN AUDREY'S. IT HAD A POOL sitting in the middle and the homes were placed in a circular fashion around it. Mel followed the numbers on the mailboxes until she reached 108. Vera didn't drive anymore, so her driveway was empty. Mel turned in and parked her car.

Before she went to the door at the side of the home, she took Deputy O'Keefe's card out of her purse and dialed his number. The call went to voicemail. She left him a message that she was going to stay with one of her grandmother's friends and wouldn't be able to see him that evening. She felt disappointed. She wasn't looking forward to an evening with Grace's friend, but she was tired and could say she wanted to go to bed early if the conversation proved too, well, boring.

Vera lived in a single-wide. She had flower boxes hanging under the front windows and neatly trimmed bushes under them. Hanging flower plants were arrayed along the edge of the roof of her carport. As Mel got out of the car, she thought she smelled pot. Maybe an evening with Vera would be more interesting than she thought.

She took out her overnight bag and left her suitcase in the car. Vera must have seen her drive in for she appeared at the door.

"Hello," she said.

"Hello," Mel said.

Vera opened the screen door and held it open. "Come in, come in."

Mel followed her through the kitchen. They walked into a small living room. A gray tabby cat sat on top of a recliner. He flicked his tail in greeting and went back to sleep.

"That's Dale. I named him after my second husband. This home only has one bedroom, so I hope you don't mind sleeping on the sofa."

"No, not at all." Especially when there's a cat in the house.

Mel put her bag on the floor next to the sofa. She smelled food, but wasn't sure if Vera had eaten already, or had made something for both of them. She sat on the sofa and waited for Vera to say something.

"Are you hungry?" Vera asked.

"Yes," Mel said. "I didn't have a chance to eat when I got here."

"I just had some soup and a sandwich. Would you like some?"

"Please."

"Come into the kitchen and I'll heat it up."

There was a tiny table pushed up against the wall with two chairs. Mel sat in one while Vera heated up the leftover soup.

"I have some ham and cheese if you'd like a sandwich," Vera said.

"No, the soup will be fine."

Mel could see steam rising from the pot of soup. It smelled good, but she couldn't discern what kind it was. She saw Vera ladle some into a large mug. As she hobbled over to the table, Mel noticed how much Vera's hands shook. She stood, reached out, and took the mug before Vera got to the table.

"Thank you," Vera said. "But I would have gotten it there."

Mel looked in the mug. It was some sort of bean soup. Not her favorite, but it would be incredibly rude to say so after Vera risked her life to bring it to her.

"Grace tells me you're here checking up on Audrey," Vera said.

"Nana hasn't heard from her in a while and got worried."

Vera made a face. "It's just like her to go off and leave people wondering what happened. She has no respect for anyone else."

Mel was surprised by Vera's words. She thought all old people liked each other, like a club or something. Vera's voice dripped with anger.

"Why do you say that?" Mel asked.

"Because I know her," Vera said. "She's not a nice person."

"Really?"

Vera nodded. "When she first came to Florida, I let her stay with me. She loved the park and decided to buy a home there."

"You lived in Holiday Oaks?"

"I did. And I was kind enough to introduce her to all my friends. Soon, she became their friend, and I became the object of their ridicule."

"That's terrible."

"Indeed. They shunned me after she came. I didn't have a friend left. It got so bad, I had to move."

"Why would she do that?"

"Because she wanted…my boyfriend."

"She stole your boyfriend?"

"She did. His name was Tom, and we had been going together for over two years. That all ended the day he met her. Brazen hussy."

Mel suppressed a smile. "Well, if he went for her like that, he wasn't a very good boyfriend."

"She turned his head. With her facelift and her tummy tuck. We all knew about her. He couldn't help himself. She was Delilah and he was Samson."

"When did this happen?" Mel asked.

"In 1997."

And she was still hurt. Wow. "I'm sorry to hear she treated you so bad."

"Badly, yes."

"Then I guess you don't know what happened to her."

"I'm not privy to what goes on in that park anymore. But I wouldn't worry about Audrey. She always took care of herself, no matter whom it hurt."

"Did you know her before she moved down here?"

"We went to high school together."

Holy crap, Mel thought. "Were you friends then?"

"I was friends with Grace."

Mel finished her soup and got up to take the mug to the sink. She rinsed it out and turned to look at Vera. "I'm kind of tired. Where's the bathroom?"

Vera used her thumb to point behind her. "It's down the hall."

Mel went to the sofa and took her toiletries out of her bag along with her sleep shirt. She had to pass Vera on her way to the bathroom and noted the miserable look on her face. It was sad that she had never gotten over what Audrey had done, if that's what Audrey had done. It seemed out of character for her to steal someone's boyfriend. It also seemed out of character for her to have plastic surgery.

When Mel came out of the bathroom, Vera was in her bedroom at the other end of the hall. Mel could hear the TV and wondered if she should stick her head in the door and say goodnight. She decided if Vera wanted to say goodnight, she would, and went to the sofa.

Before turning off the lights, she pulled out her phone. She had a text message from Deputy O'Keefe saying he'd gotten her message. He asked her to meet him in the parking lot at the sheriff's office in the morning around ten. He signed it "Conner."

Mel called Laura to tell her she'd arrived safely, but Laura didn't pick up her phone. Mel left a message on her voicemail and hung up.

She looked at the time on her phone. It was eight o'clock. She couldn't believe she was going to bed so early. Maybe it had something to do with spending the night in an over fifty-five park. Maybe something in the air made everyone go to bed early.

WHEN SHE WOKE THE NEXT MORNING, THE GRAY TABBY WAS asleep on her chest. She pushed it off and it protested, then she got up and brushed cat hair off her sleep shirt. She glanced at the clock on Vera's cable box. It read seven. She had slept for eleven hours.

Vera was at the kitchen table and saluted her with her coffee cup.

"Good morning," she said.

"Hi," Mel said.

"You slept well. I slept well when I was your age. That's the curse of old age. Now that you have the time to sleep in, you can't."

"I was wiped out. Is there more coffee?"

"I made a whole pot. I usually don't, but I thought you might like some."

Mel went to the counter where the ancient Mr. Coffee sat. Vera had put a mug next to it for her and she filled it.

"Milk and sugar are on the table," Vera said.

Mel sat and put sugar in her coffee. Vera seemed to have something on her mind.

"I'm sorry for the things I said last night," she said.

"Oh, don't worry about it."

"I do worry about it. I tend to live in the past and I promised myself this new year I would stop."

"Well, you have a few more days yet to make that resolution."

"True, but I still should have been more considerate. She is your aunt after all. And she has some good points."

"What are they?"

"She is very intelligent. She is one of the most interesting people I've ever met. She had traveled all over the country."

"Really? I don't think Nana Grace ever left New Jersey."

"No, she didn't. Grace was happy to stay put. I always asked her to come and visit, but she always declined."

"I appreciate you letting me stay here. I don't know what I would have done if you hadn't. The hotels are all booked."

"Christmas vacation is upon us. People are here getting a head start on the season."

"I know. A friend of mine is staying at a condo in

Clearwater Beach. She asked me to join her, but until I find out what happened to Audrey, I can't."

"What do you think happened to her?"

"I don't want to talk about what I think happened."

"Have you been to her home?"

"Yesterday. And some guy is living there. He's way too young for her."

Vera narrowed her eyes. "Vera preferred men her own age. She was never one to chase after gigolos."

"I don't think he's a gigolo, but I'm not sure what he is."

"What did he say when you asked where she was?"

"He said she went on a cruise to Europe."

"Alone?"

"No. With a friend from another park."

"It's possible. Don't you need a passport to travel to Europe?" Vera asked.

"I don't know. I guess you would, though, since you're going over water that isn't part of the United States."

"I may be wrong, but I don't think Audrey had a passport."

"You said she traveled a lot."

"Yes, in the United States. There was something about her birth certificate. Oh, I wish I could remember."

"Nana mentioned something about that, too."

"Yes. Grace would have had the same problem. Maybe that's why she never traveled."

"That's what she said. They were both born in Cuba."

"They were twins."

"They were!" Mel cried. "She didn't mention that."

"Oh, yes. I grew up with them. We were in the same classes in high school. They were fraternal twins."

"I wonder why nobody told me that?"

Vera shook her head. "I don't know."

"I'm gonna call my grandmother," Mel said. She got up, took her phone off the charger, went to the door, and went outside. She dialed Grace's number, then changed her mind and hung up. She still hadn't told Grace that she hadn't found Audrey. She dialed Laura instead.

"Hello," Laura said.

"Hi, Grandma. It's Mel."

"Hi, Mel. It's early for you to call."

"I know. I went to bed early."

"Where are you?"

"I'm at Nana's friend's house. Vera. We just had coffee. Listen, Grandma, Vera told me Nana and Audrey are twins."

"That's right."

"How come I didn't know that?"

"You didn't? I don't know. Maybe it just didn't come up."

"But that's the kind of thing I should know, don't you think?"

"Mel, is it really that important?"

"It may be. Vera thought of something. Can you tell me more about their birth certificates?"

"I don't know more than I told you already."

"You said there was a glitch."

"Yes, but I can't remember exactly what it was."

"How can we ask Nana without tipping her off that Audrey is missing?"

"I could ask her about it. It's not a big secret."

"But won't she wonder why you're bringing it up now?"

"Did you talk to her yet?" Laura asked.

"Yesterday. I said Audrey was out when I went there."

"So she doesn't know someone else is living there."

"No. I thought we'd find her before I had to."

"I agree. She'd just worry." Laura paused. "Thanks for this, Mel. She really appreciates it. That dream upset her. She's very worried about her sister."

Mel felt a tug at her heart. "I know. I'm gonna find out where she is."

"I hope so."

"I'm meeting a deputy this morning who has promised to help me."

"Oh, that's good."

"And there's a neighbor there I want to talk to. I'll let you know what happens."

"And I'll try to keep a positive outlook."

"Tell her I'm thinking about her."

"I will. You be careful down there this time of year."

"I will. See ya, Grandma."

"Bye, dear."

Mel hung up the phone and looked at the patch of grass at the side of Vera's house. The sun was out. It was a beautiful day.

Mel thought about her grandmother and aunt being born in Cuba. She was amazed that she had never heard about that before, nor the fact that they were twins. She had to ask Conner where she would find out about an application for a passport.

She went back inside and Vera was scrambling eggs.

"Do you want some?" she asked.

"Sure," Mel said.

Vera took a plate out of the cabinet and filled it with eggs. "The toast is on the table."

When Mel began eating, she realized how hungry she was, and her plate was empty within minutes.

"That was good," she said. "Thanks."

"Glad you enjoyed it."

"I have to meet somebody at ten. I think I'll get dressed."

"Who are you meeting?"

"A deputy. He's gonna help me find out what happened to Audrey."

"Are you coming back later?" Vera looked concerned.

"I'm not sure. Can I call you later and let you know?"

"I'll be here."

Mel walked over to Vera and put her arm around the old woman's shoulders. "I really do appreciate this."

"I know. It's just nice having someone to talk to."

Again, Mel felt a tug at her heart. "I have to see how things go today."

Mel retrieved her bag and took it into the bathroom. She emerged fully dressed and went to the sofa to collect her things.

"I'm gonna take a ride over to Holiday Oaks," she said. "Maybe I'll see you later."

She walked over to Vera, who was sitting at the kitchen table with her second cup of coffee, and gave her a hug.

"Be careful on the roads," Vera said. "Crazy drivers are out there this time of year."

"I'll be careful."

Mel left the home and got into her car. It was eight-thirty. Most old people were up early, right? She wanted to see the lady who lived across the street from Audrey. If she sat there every day, she might have seen something. She also might have seen Audrey with Jason, and Mel was going to find out why her aunt would let Jason into her life.

Chapter Six

When Mel drove up, the woman was sitting on the porch with her yapping dog. Mel got out of the car, walked up to her, and the dog barked louder.

"Hi," Mel said. "I wonder if I could talk to you for a minute?"

The woman stared at her. "Shut up, Maurice!" she cried. "Yes? What do you want?"

"I was wondering if you'd seen my aunt, Audrey Glenn, lately?"

The woman smiled. "So, somebody finally came to check on her. I saw you yesterday, then I saw the cop. You could have just asked me then."

"A cop was here?"

"Big fella in a sheriff's car."

Conner hadn't mentioned he'd stopped by. The dog's barking was beginning to annoy Mel. Every few seconds it would stop and sniff, then start barking again.

"Did you know Audrey well?"

"Not to talk to, no. She wasn't very friendly if you ask me. Just hung around with those biddies at the pool.

Gossip mongers, that's all they were, just gossip mongers. Liked to hurt people. Talked about 'em and made up lies."

"Have you seen her lately?" Mel asked again.

"No."

"How long has that younger guy been living there?"

"He showed up about five months ago. I keep a notebook. I like to keep track of things, especially strangers. I looked at it yesterday when you came around. I knew you had to be a relative. You look like her."

No one had ever said that to Mel before. "Really?"

"Younger, but still like her."

"Did she ever say anything to you about him?"

"Listen, honey, like I said, we didn't talk. Shut up, Maurice! Damn dog. He never used to bark like this. All the sudden he starts and I can't get him to stop."

Mel looked at the dog. "When did he start barking?"

"I'd have to look in my notebook again. Stay here."

The woman got up, grabbed her cane, and went into the house through a sliding glass door, leaving it open. She appeared a minute later with a ring-bound notebook. She returned to her seat and opened it.

"Says here he started yapping in September."

Three months ago. "I didn't catch your name."

"I'm Marge. Marge Winthrop."

"Well, Ms. Winthrop, if you hear anything, please call me. Can you put my number in your notebook?" Marge had a pen inside the rings of the notebook and pulled it out. "My name is Mel Jones, and my number is 732-555-0645."

"That isn't a local number."

"No, it isn't."

"I guess it's okay. But only if I hear something. I'm not gonna be your new phone buddy."

That's good. "Have a good day."

Mel drove away and went around the park to the office. She wondered when the "gossip mongers" came to the pool. She parked in the visitor's lot where she had a view of the pool. There were several older women in lounge chairs sitting there. Mel got out of the car and walked over to the gate in the chain link enclosure surrounding the pool. She went through it and walked up to the women.

"Hi," she said, and all heads turned her way. "I'm Audrey Glenn's niece. I was wondering if any of you knew her."

"We all do," one of them said. She had a deep tan and the wrinkles to prove she had spent way too much time in the sun.

"Do you know where she is?" Mel asked.

"Only what that boy told us, that she went on a cruise."

"Do you believe she went on a cruise?"

Mel counted them. There were six women altogether. Three of them didn't speak, but they all looked at each other and then at Mel.

"She never said she was going anywhere," the one in the middle said.

"When was the last time she sat with you?"

"I saw her a few months ago," a redhead said. "It must have been September."

"That's right," the tanned lady said. "I remember now. She was talking about that boy. He didn't like to sit with us so she got to talk about him. She wanted him to move out."

"That's right," a blonde said. "She was going to ask him to leave. He was eating too much food and asking her for money all the time."

"I told her when she let him move in it was a bad mistake," the redhead said. "But he was nice to her, and I think Audrey was lonely."

43

"Do you think he would hurt her?" Mel asked.

Silence. They looked at each other again. Then the tanned lady spoke.

"He's young, but he didn't seem mean. He was here with her a few times, and he seemed very attentive."

"I never trusted him," the redhead said.

"You never trust anybody," the blonde said. "Look, sweetie, Audrey never listened to anyone. She did what she wanted to do. We all thought letting him live there was a bad idea. I mean, he could have been a gigolo. But she liked him and she wouldn't listen to us."

"And you haven't seen her in three months?" They all shook their heads. "And none of you went over there to see if she was all right?"

They all cast their eyes to the ground, then the tanned lady looked at Mel.

"You're young. You don't understand what it's like to be older. If he hurt her, and we went snooping around, he might hurt one of us. He knows where we live."

"Then why didn't one of you call the police?"

Their silence implied the same thought – they didn't want to get involved. Mel was getting angry. So many people hadn't seen Audrey in months, and no one asked why.

Mel walked away. She wanted to yell something obscene at them, but what good would it do? Marge was right – they were a bunch of gossip mongers, not friends. Maybe that's why Audrey invited Jason into her life, because he pretended to be her friend.

Mel pulled out her phone and looked at the time. It was nine-thirty. She could go to the sheriff's office parking lot and wait for Conner.

Chapter Seven

Mel parked near the front of the parking lot so Conner could see her. She watched the cruisers driving in and out of the lot, some with backseat passengers, some without. She wondered if Jason had ever been a backseat passenger in a cruiser. She'd have to ask Conner to look him up.

She pulled out her notepad. She had jotted down some questions for Conner. Number one was about the passport. Where would Audrey apply? If she had applied, it would lend credence to Jason's assertion that she had gone on a cruise. If not, Mel would know he was lying.

Conner arrived on the dot of ten and parked behind her car. He wasn't in uniform. Mel got out and went to him.

"You want to take my car?" he said.

"It's easier. You know where you're going. Just let me get my bag."

She grabbed her purse and locked the doors on the rental, then she got into Conner's 2008 Toyota. She was surprised to find it so clean as most of the guys she'd dated accumulated junk in their cars. They usually had to clear a space for her to sit on.

"Have you eaten?" he asked.

"Two hours ago. I could eat something."

"I need coffee. Let's go to Panera's."

The Panera Bread was located in the Largo Mall just down the street from the sheriff's office. Conner got a parking spot nearby and they went inside. He got a large coffee and an Elephant Ear and she got a medium coffee and a banana nut muffin. They found a table next to the window and sat down.

"I went to Holiday Oaks this morning," she said.

"I went yesterday."

"I know. The old lady across the street from Audrey's told me."

"So much for stealth reconnaissance."

"You'd never get past her. I think she sleeps out there."

"Did she have anything new to add?"

Mel thought about their conversation. "She didn't like Audrey very much. She also said the guy moved in there about five months ago. She keeps a record of everything that goes on around her in a notebook. Oh, and she said her dog started barking about three months ago. Apparently, he didn't before."

"Three months."

"Yeah. Do you think it means anything?" Mel had her own ideas, but nothing she wanted to think about.

"It could mean he smells something he doesn't like. Some strong smell."

"Oh." She looked at her hands. She looked upset.

"That doesn't mean it's a body. He could smell a dead rat. Dogs can smell anything. And it doesn't have to be close."

"A rat?" Mel said.

"Yeah. There's water behind that park. They live there. They like to get the grapefruit that falls off the trees."

"Oh, God."

"I take it you don't have rats where you come from?"

"Not in my backyard, no. Mice maybe."

"Did she say anything else?" Conner asked.

"No. I went to the pool and talked to some women there. They said Audrey hadn't been to the pool since September. They didn't seem too concerned, which pissed me off."

"Why?"

"Marge said they were her friends."

"I think older people define friendship differently than we do," Conner said.

"I don't think so. I just think that group, well, they reminded me of the mean girls in school, only old. Real polite, but totally disinterested in Audrey's welfare."

Conner reached out and put his hand on hers. "We'll find her."

"Why didn't anyone check on her?" Mel asked. "How could she be out of sight for so long without someone asking why?"

"They would have if she hadn't paid the rent."

"I asked the woman at the office and she said she'd been paying her rent with money orders."

"That wouldn't leave a trail. It wouldn't matter who signed them."

"I wonder if she gets a check in the mail every month from Social Security," Mel said.

"I don't think they get checks anymore. I think they have to have direct deposit. At least someone like Audrey would. She's lived in the same place a long time. She had to have a checking account."

"And to get the money out, someone would need her

signature on a check, right?"

"Not if she had a debit card." Conner said.

"That's right. Shit."

They ate in silence for a while, and when they were done, took their plates to the counter and left.

"Where do you want to start?" Conner asked.

"I want to find out if she had a passport."

"Then let's go see the Clerk of Court."

They drove to Court Street. The county courthouse there was home to civil cases. Conner knew some of the clerks and knew this courthouse wasn't as busy as the criminal one on 49th Street. He parked in a paid lot across the street and put in enough coins for an hour.

They walked inside and Mel was disappointed. She thought it would be more interesting. It looked like any other office building.

She followed Conner down a hallway and to a window that had the sign "Clerk" over it. A pleasant looking woman came to slide the window open when she saw Conner standing there.

"Hey," she said. "How are you?"

"I'm good."

"You're here on your day off?" she asked, noting his civilian clothes.

"Yes, Ma'am. Penny, this is Mel. We were wondering if you could help us."

"If I can, sure."

"Mel's aunt may have applied for a passport recently, say, within the last three months. Is there any way to look that up?"

"I can look up the application, but that's about it. It goes to another department and they aren't as nice as I am." She smiled, then turned and went back to her desk. "What's the name?"

"Audrey Glenn," he shouted.

Penny typed something into her keyboard. "I don't see any applications in here. I'm gonna go back farther."

Penny went back a year and still came up empty. Conner looked at Mel.

"She didn't apply for one in this county," he said.

"Then he's lying," Mel said.

Penny came to the window with a sheet of paper she printed out. "She did apply for a new driver's license. She didn't follow through, though. She was rejected for her eyesight. All she needed were corrective lenses. I guess she didn't like wearing glasses."

"What about the registration on her car?" Conner asked. He had seen the Mercury when he stopped at the home.

"I didn't check that. Wait."

Penny went back to her desk. She looked up registrations under Audrey's name. "She was due on her birthday, September 2, but she didn't apply. Let me look up the VIN." Penny searched for registrations by vehicle identification number. "The car is registered to a Jason Frye. Do you know him?"

"Shit," Mel said. "He's got her car."

"What about her mobile home registration?" Conner asked. "Can you find it with her name?"

"I should be able to," Penny said. Penny typed for several minutes. "I got it." She then typed some more. "It was transferred to the same guy, Jason Frye. He's the registered owner of the mobile home."

"But how can that be? It's an over fifty-five park."

Penny did another search. "According to this, Jason Frye is sixty-two-years-old."

"Bullshit he is," Mel said.

"He's a kid, Penny. There's no way he's sixty-two."

"He would have had to get the park's approval before the transfer of ownership," Penny said. "That would mean a credit check. I know because I just moved my mom into that park. They are pretty careful about who gets in."

"Thanks, Penny. I'll bring you a mocha Frappuccino the next time I come in."

"I'll hold you to that," Penny said with a smile. "I just thought of something." She went back to her desk.

"That son of a bitch stole her house and her car," Mel said. "We can't let him get away with this."

Penny printed something out. "I printed out the title. The original with Audrey's name on it. It has both signatures on it." She brought it over and gave it to Conner.

"Can you print out a copy of her DL with the signature on it?" he asked.

"Yeah," Penny said, going back to her desk. She found it, printed it out, and brought it to him. He and Mel looked at it.

"That's not Audrey's signature," Mel said. "It's totally different from the one on her license."

"That would be fraud," Penny said.

"Thanks for your help," Conner said.

"Anytime."

They left the courthouse and got into the car. Mel was fuming. She wanted to hang Jason by his testicles. Conner was comparing signatures on the driver's license and the title transfers.

"You're right," Conner said. "Your aunt didn't sign this title transfer."

Mel looked at them again. The signature on the driver's license looked similar to Grace's handwriting, neat and perfectly executed. The signature on the title transfers looked like Mel's, sloppy and illegible. At a glance, she knew her aunt hadn't signed them.

Chapter Eight

CONNER WAS KEEPING HIS TRUE THOUGHTS ABOUT AUDREY to himself. He remembered finding an older Jason Frye and knew he had to be the one who signed the titles. As they sat in the sheriff's parking lot, Conner scrolled through the "Who's in Jail" page on the sheriff's website. The older one was sixty-two. The other was thirty. Both had been in jail on possession charges. He assumed they were father and son, and the elder Frye had helped the younger swindle Audrey out of her home and car. He jotted down the address for the older Frye.

"What's the plan?" Mel asked.

"We are going to find Jason Frye."

"We already did."

"The other one. The older one."

"You think there is another one?" she asked.

"I know there is." He showed her his phone. "I think they're father and son."

"It would make more sense. Audrey might go for a guy over sixty. But why isn't he living in her house? Everyone I talked to said the younger guy has been living with her."

"That's what I want to find out."

They got out of the car and went inside to his desk. She sat in the chair in front of his desk while he did a search for Jason Frye, Sr. He had been bailed out of jail in 2011. Conner couldn't find any more information on him.

"You got that printout Penny gave you?"

"Yeah," she said. She pulled it out of her purse and handed it to him.

"The transaction was in 2013. The back of the title is signed. We need something with the younger Frye's signature."

"His driver's license would have it."

"I forgot to ask Penny for that. "

She slumped a bit in the seat.

"It's gonna be all right," he said.

"Do you think he…hurt her?"

Conner hesitated. "I never jump to conclusions."

"Even when they are slapping you in the face?"

"Especially then."

She sighed. "I just want to know what happened to her. I don't believe she's on any cruise."

Conner again put his hand on hers.

"I've done these kinds of cases before. It's very possible she did go on a cruise. Don't give up on her yet."

Mel nodded, but the feeling in her gut didn't go away.

Conner turned on the engine. He didn't put the car in gear, though.

"Where are we going now?" she asked.

"I'm hungry," he said.

"So do you want to get something to eat?"

"Do you mind?"

"No. I'll eat something."

He took her to a taco place on Starkey Road. The tacos were huge and tasted good. Mel kept looking at

Conner. He was a nice guy. He was good looking. Too bad he lived in Florida.

"Both Jason and his father were arrested for possession. I didn't see that either of them did any jail time, so they must have pled out at arraignment and were sentenced to probation and fines."

"Was that the only time they were arrested?"

"In Pinellas County. I didn't find either of them on the FDLE website. That means they didn't go to prison." He wiped his mouth. "I want to know where the dad is."

"He would have had to be around to get the title changed over, right? The people in the park office would have wanted to see him, wouldn't they?"

"You'd think so. But these guys may be slick enough to fool them, too."

"The woman I met in the office had to be seventy. They might have caught her off-guard."

"Is she the one who signs the leases?"

"I don't think so. She wasn't the manager. She did know how the rent was being paid, though."

"She probably covers the office for the manager. We gotta talk to them." He looked at her empty wrapper. "You finished?"

"Yeah. Let's go."

They got into his car and she sighed.

"I keep seeing her in a hospital, or nursing home."

"They would have contacted her family."

"Would they? What if Jason took her there? What if she was unconscious and he gave them her emergency contacts?"

Conner would be glad if they found Audrey in a nursing home. At least she would be alive.

"Be glad if we find her that way," he said.

"What other way…oh. I can't think about that."

"We forgot to get something else from Penny."

"What?"

"A copy of the new titles. The ones showing Jason Frye as the owner. We're closer to the DMV. We can stop there and I'll get copies."

The DMV was crowded. They got a number and waited until it was called. They went to the desk and Conner smiled at the woman and flashed his badge.

"I was wondering if you could help me," he said.

"In an official capacity?" the woman asked. Her name badge said "Connie."

"Ah, yes. I need current titles for someone named Jason Frye."

She began to type. "Is there a middle name?"

He went back to Jason, Jr.'s mug shot on his phone. "John."

She typed for a minute. "July 8, 1952."

"That's the father," Mel said.

"Wait, there's two," Connie said. "The other one is January 5, 1980."

"Are they both on the title?" Conner asked.

"No. And I can't tell which one did the transfer," Connie said. "The middle initial is the same, and the title doesn't have junior or senior listed."

"Shit," Mel said under her breath.

"What's the address on their DLs?" Conner asked.

She typed. "It's the same on both."

Connie printed out the information and slid it across the desk. The address was the same as Audrey's mobile home.

"Does that tell you when they got them?"

"Date of issue is September 2," Connie said.

"Didn't Penny say that was when the registration was due?" Mel asked.

"Didn't they need some sort of ID to register the home?" Conner asked.

"Yes, they would have to show their driver's license or a utility bill with their name on it, but not for the seller, only for the buyer."

"Can you print the original paperwork they brought in?" Mel asked.

"I'm not sure," Connie said. Conner smiled.

"It would really help us," he said.

"Ah, okay." Connie scrolled through the papers Jason Frye brought in when he registered the home. They had been scanned into the computer. She printed out the application and a copy of a driver's license.

Conner and Mel looked at the signature at the bottom of the application and the signature on the driver's license. Jason Frye, Jr. had signed the application. Now they knew it was Jason, Jr. who had forged Audrey's signature on the title transfer.

"We may have probable cause for a warrant," Conner said.

"Really?" Mel said.

"Really. Can I have a copy of the older Frye's DL?"

Connie printed out a copy of the older Frye's driver's license and slid it across the desk.

After they left the DMV, Conner was quiet. He was going over the clues in his head. If he had doubts about whether Audrey was dead or alive before, he didn't anymore.

"I can't believe they got away with this," Mel said.

"They haven't yet," Conner said. "I'm still wondering where the old man is. I didn't see him at the home the other day."

"Me either."

When they got to the car, Conner took out the paperwork they had just collected and looked at all the signatures.

"There are two distinctly different signatures," he said. "The kid signed as Audrey."

"Let's go talk to the manager of the park. They would have had to meet the man buying the home, right? To see if he was old enough?"

"And the lease would have his signature on it. Good thinking."

Mel blushed and smiled. She was warming up to Conner in a big way.

The lobby in the park office had been decorated for the season and a large Christmas tree stood in the center. Mel hadn't noticed it the day before and when she saw it, she sighed.

"I wish I was home for Christmas," she said. "My grandmother will miss me."

"Maybe we'll get this wrapped up by then," Conner said.

There was another older woman sitting at the desk.

"Can I help you?" she said.

"Can I speak to the manager?" Mel asked.

"Maybe I can help you," the woman said.

"No, I have to see the manager."

The woman frowned and pushed herself away from the desk. She made a show of getting up, grunting and sighing, then walked to a door. She went inside, then came back and sat down.

"Give her a minute," she said.

Mel and Conner stood in front of the desk until a younger woman appeared at the door to the office.

"Hi," she said. "I'm Nancy. How can I help you?"

"Can we go into your office?" Conner asked. He flashed his badge.

"Sure."

She took them to her office and closed the door. There were two chairs in front of another gray metal desk and they sat while she took her seat behind it.

"Now," she said. "What can I do for you?"

"My aunt owns a home here. Her name is Audrey Glenn. We haven't heard from her in a while, and now I found some guy living in her house."

"Really," Nancy said. "Which number?"

"298," Mel said.

Nancy typed and pulled up the info for 298. "That home is owned by a Jason Frye. This lists the previous owner as Audrey Glenn."

"When did she sell the trailer?" Conner asked.

"They are manufactured homes," Nancy said, with a slight edge in her voice.

"When did she sell the home?" he said.

"September. I've only been here for two months. My predecessor handled the transaction. She didn't keep very good records, which is why she no longer works here. I've spent a lot of time cleaning things up."

"Have you met Jason Frye?" Mel asked. "He's like thirty."

"That's impossible," Nancy said. "Even the former manager couldn't have allowed a man that age to sign a lease. The actual owner has to be over fifty-five."

"But does that mean someone under fifty-five can live there alone?"

"No. Unless it was temporary. We have rules. Even a widow under fifty-five has to leave, unless she's close to fifty-five. We have made some exceptions, but they're rare."

"I've got news for you, lady," Mel said. "That guy is living there alone and he's not fifty-five."

Conner put a hand on Mel, who looked as if she wanted to grab Nancy by the throat.

"Do you have a copy of the lease Jason Frye signed?" Conner asked.

Nancy pushed herself away from her desk and rolled over to a filing cabinet directly behind her. She looked through some files and found the lease for 298. She rolled back to the desk and handed it to Conner. He pulled out the driver's licenses for the Fryes and compared them to the lease.

"It's the old man," he said. "He signed the lease."

"Have you ever met Jason Frye?" Mel asked Nancy.

"No, I'm afraid not. I've been so busy since taking over I haven't had a chance to meet all the residents. There are over six hundred, you know."

"No, I didn't know. Thank you for telling me."

"Can I have a copy of this?" Conner asked.

"Sure," Nancy said. She got up and went to the all-in-one printer on the bookcase next to the filing cabinet and made him a copy of the lease. When she handed it to him, she held it.

"Are you sure there was no one over fifty-five living there?" she asked Conner.

"Not absolutely sure, but the younger guy was alone when I went there yesterday."

"The owner could have been out," Nancy said.

"The car was in the driveway," Conner said.

"He could have been at the pool," Nancy said.

"Why don't you go over there and see for yourself?" Mel asked.

"Thanks, Nancy," Conner said. He stood and looked at Mel. She stood, and then followed him out the door.

"I didn't like her," Mel said. "She's full of shit."

"Yes, but we may need her. It's always better to keep them on your side."

"Do you believe the old guy ever lived there? I mean, wouldn't someone have mentioned him? Marge never said anything about an older man, and neither did the old man or the mean girl women I talked to."

"Maybe we should talk to Marge together," Conner said.

"She's always on the porch," Mel said.

Chapter Nine

THE SKY HAD GROWN CLOUDY WHILE THEY WERE IN THE office.

"It's gonna rain," Conner said.

Marge was at her station on the porch and Maurice was barking.

"Shut up, Maurice," Marge yelled when she saw them pull up. She recognized Mel and Conner from the day before.

"Hi, Marge," Mel said as they walked up to the porch. "This is Deputy O'Keefe. He wanted to ask you some questions."

"Deputy, huh? It's about time one of you came to talk to me."

"Any particular reason we should be talking to you?" Conner asked.

"The girl knows. We talked this morning."

"Marge," Mel said. "Have you ever seen another man living in my aunt's house?"

"What do you mean?" Marge asked.

"An older man, say, around sixty," Conner said.

"No. Just the kid. I complained to Bea about it."

"Who's Bea?" Conner asked.

"The manager," Marge said.

"The manager's name is Nancy," Mel said.

"Not that one, the one before. I told her that kid didn't belong here. He was doing something to annoy Maurice and I wanted him out."

"What did she say?" Conner asked.

"She said what she always said, that she'd look into it. The woman never did a damn thing the whole time she was here."

Conner was watching the dog. He kept sniffing, then barking, and his eyes were trained on something across the street.

"How long has Maurice been barking?" Conner said.

"Three months."

"And you're sure you've never seen an older man living there?"

"I've never seen anyone but that boy. Are you gonna do something to get him out?"

"We're working on it," Conner said. "Thanks for your help."

"Yeah," Marge said. "You're working on it."

"Bye, Marge," Mel said.

They went back to the car and Conner took out his notebook. Mel watched Audrey's home as he filled in his notes.

"Why would a dog bark when he didn't before?" she asked. "What would make him do that?"

"He was sniffing a lot," Conner said. "He smells something he doesn't like."

"Coming from my aunt's house?"

Conner nodded. "We have to get inside again, but I'd

rather do it with a warrant. If we find something, we have to be able to use it later on."

Mel started crying. "I didn't even know her."

"She's still family. And, how old was she?"

"She was in her nineties."

For the third time since they met in the parking lot that morning, Conner put his hand on hers. She liked the way it felt. "You have a right to be concerned. She was pretty old."

"She wouldn't have been able to fight him off."

"Are you hungry?" he asked.

Mel smiled. "Again? Really? No, I'm not."

"Well, I could go for some ice cream." Conner started the car and backed out of the street, turned left, and drove to Ulmerton Road. "There's a creamery place in the mall."

Mel did order a chocolate chip cone. It took her mind off Audrey for a few minutes, that and watching Conner eat a banana split.

"That was good," he said, wiping fudge off his mouth. "I think I'm gonna go to my office and see if I can get a warrant."

"Can I go with you?" Mel asked.

"Why don't you go see your friend in Clearwater? I'll call you if they agree to a warrant."

"She's probably on the beach right now," Mel said.

"But she has a phone with her, right?"

"Yeah, she should."

"Call her. It'll be good for you to see someone else for a few hours."

But I like being with you, she thought. "Okay. You promise you'll call me?"

"As soon as I know. Hey, give me the paperwork you've got."

She pulled the papers she had out of her purse and put

them on the seat. He dropped her off at her car. She waved as he pulled away. When she got into her car, she dialed Lisa.

"Hey, it's me," Mel said.

"Where are you? I thought you were coming today."

"I got stuck here. My aunt is missing."

"Well that sucks."

"A nice cop is helping me. I have a little time while he works on something and thought I'd come over."

"Great. I'm on the beach, but you'll never find us. I'll go back to the condo so I can bring you over."

"Who's with you?"

"A friend from work, Sandy."

"Oh, okay. I'll see you in a few."

Mel pulled up the GPS on her iPhone. It had the condo address on it so all she had to do was touch the screen and follow it to Clearwater Beach.

Chapter Ten

THE SKY HAD GROWN CLOUDY WHILE THEY WERE IN THE office.

"It's gonna rain," Conner said.

Marge was at her station on the porch and Maurice was barking.

"Shut up, Maurice," Marge yelled when she saw them pull up. She recognized Mel and Conner from the day before.

"Hi, Marge," Mel said as they walked up to the porch. "This is Deputy O'Keefe. He wanted to ask you some questions."

"Deputy, huh? It's about time one of you came to talk to me."

"Any particular reason we should be talking to you?" Conner asked.

"The girl knows. We talked this morning."

"Marge," Mel said. "Have you ever seen another man living in my aunt's house?"

"What do you mean?" Marge asked.

"An older man, say, around sixty," Conner said.

"No. Just the kid. I complained to Bea about it."

"Who's Bea?" Conner asked.

"The manager," Marge said.

"The manager's name is Nancy," Mel said.

"Not that one, the one before. I told her that kid didn't belong here. He was doing something to annoy Maurice and I wanted him out."

"What did she say?" Conner asked.

"She said what she always said, that she'd look into it. The woman never did a damn thing the whole time she was here."

Conner was watching the dog. He kept sniffing, then barking, and his eyes were trained on something across the street.

"How long has Maurice been barking?" Conner said.

"Three months."

"And you're sure you've never seen an older man living there?"

"I've never seen anyone but that boy. Are you gonna do something to get him out?"

"We're working on it," Conner said. "Thanks for your help."

"Yeah," Marge said. "You're working on it."

"Bye, Marge," Mel said.

They went back to the car and Conner took out his notebook. Mel watched Audrey's home as he filled in his notes.

"Why would a dog bark when he didn't before?" she asked. "What would make him do that?"

"He was sniffing a lot," Conner said. "He smells something he doesn't like."

"Coming from my aunt's house?"

Conner nodded. "We have to get inside again, but I'd

rather do it with a warrant. If we find something, we have to be able to use it later on."

Mel started crying. "I didn't even know her."

"She's still family. And, how old was she?"

"She was in her nineties."

For the third time since they met in the parking lot that morning, Conner put his hand on hers. She liked the way it felt. "You have a right to be concerned. She was pretty old."

"She wouldn't have been able to fight him off."

"Are you hungry?" he asked.

Mel smiled. "Again? Really? No, I'm not."

"Well, I could go for some ice cream." Conner started the car and backed out of the street, turned left, and drove to Ulmerton Road. "There's a creamery place in the mall."

Mel did order a chocolate chip cone. It took her mind off Audrey for a few minutes, that and watching Conner eat a banana split.

"That was good," he said, wiping fudge off his mouth. "I think I'm gonna go to my office and see if I can get a warrant."

"Can I go with you?" Mel asked.

"Why don't you go see your friend in Clearwater? I'll call you if they agree to a warrant."

"She's probably on the beach right now," Mel said.

"But she has a phone with her, right?"

"Yeah, she should."

"Call her. It'll be good for you to see someone else for a few hours."

But I like being with you, she thought. "Okay. You promise you'll call me?"

"As soon as I know. Hey, give me the paperwork you've got."

She pulled the papers she had out of her purse and put

them on the seat. He dropped her off at her car. She waved as he pulled away. When she got into her car, she dialed Lisa.

"Hey, it's me," Mel said.

"Where are you? I thought you were coming today."

"I got stuck here. My aunt is missing."

"Well that sucks."

"A nice cop is helping me. I have a little time while he works on something and thought I'd come over."

"Great. I'm on the beach, but you'll never find us. I'll go back to the condo so I can bring you over."

"Who's with you?"

"A friend from work, Sandy."

"Oh, okay. I'll see you in a few."

Mel pulled up the GPS on her iPhone. It had the condo address on it so all she had to do was touch the screen and follow it to Clearwater Beach.

Mel dialed Lisa's number again. She was standing in front of the condo, but Lisa was nowhere in sight. She checked the time on her phone – it was three. She paced. The call went straight to voicemail.

"Don't tell me you're missing, too," Mel said. She hung up and continued to pace the sidewalk. A minute later, Conner called.

"Hey, I had the handwriting checked out. It's definitely the kid who signed the title to the home."

"Can you arrest him?" she asked.

"I need more."

"What more do you need?" she said. She was growing frustrated. "You have proof that he signed her title."

"But I'm not working as a deputy. I have to bring this to my supervisor and see if he'll okay an investigation."

"So what are you waiting for?" she asked.

Conner rolled his eyes. "I'm waiting for something more definitive. She could have been incapacitated and asked him to sign for her. We don't know what happened yet."

"Sorry. I keep forgetting you're on my side."

"I'm gonna check out the last address of Jason senior. It's in Clearwater. I thought maybe you would like to join me. That is, if you're free."

Mel looked up and down the sidewalk. She didn't see Lisa. She wanted to go with Conner.

"Okay. I have to leave a message for my friend. Where should I meet you?"

"There's a Publix on Gulf-to-Bay near Belcher Road. Don't rush. There's a lot of traffic. I'll wait if I get there first."

She hung up and dialed Lisa's number. It went straight to voicemail again.

"Hey, Lisa, I waited but you never showed. I have to go with the cop to another place so I guess I'll talk to you tomorrow." She hesitated before hanging up. "I hope you're okay."

Conner was right – the traffic sucked. It was stop and go all the way up Gulf-to-Bay. It was a major shopping area and Christmas was getting closer every day. The roads wouldn't get better until January.

She found the Publix and turned into the parking lot. Conner had parked near the end where she would be sure to see him. He smiled and put up his hand in a sort of wave when she parked next to him. She rolled down the window.

"Do you want to use my car again?" he asked.

"You know where we're going."

She got out and then got into his car. They headed to the last known address of Jason Frye Sr. It was a mobile home park that had seen better days.

The park had been a nice over fifty-five park in the sixties. The homes were actual trailers – small and placed close to each other. Now, fifty years later, it was a rundown park in a bad part of town. The houses were rusty and the yards unkempt. It was home to drug users and the other dregs of society.

"This place is scary," Mel said.

"It's just old. It was probably nice once."

They found the manager's office and parked in front of it. It was a small house near the community center. The door was locked and Conner knocked.

A younger woman answered the door. She smiled.

"Hi," she said.

"Hello, ma'am." Conner showed her his badge. "Can I ask you about one of your residents?"

"Sure," she said.

"His name is Jason Frye. This park is his last known address."

She looked smug. "I'm surprised you don't know."

"Don't know what?" Conner asked.

"That he died. Must be three months ago already."

Mel looked at Conner. His expression never changed.

"Is there someone occupying his home?" Conner asked.

"No. It still has the yellow tape across the entrance."

"The police investigated?"

"They had to. They thought he might have been murdered."

If Conner was surprised, he never showed it.

"Could you tell me where the home is?"

She pointed down the road. "It's the third one down. 189 I think. He stunk to high heaven. That's why I called the police. The home may still smell bad. Just an FYI."

They walked away and headed down the road.

"How long could he have been there if he smelled bad?" Mel asked.

"It doesn't take long in the heat," Conner said. "It could have been a couple of days. That lease was signed in September. It could have been right after that."

"So you think junior did it?"

"It crossed my mind, but if he had, they would have arrested him by now. He'd be the number one suspect."

They found the number they were looking for, but they didn't need it – the crime scene tape gave it away. The trailer had an old, screened in porch and the tape ran across the door. Conner pulled it down.

"Won't you get into trouble for doing that?" Mel asked.

"We can put it back up."

There was powder residue on the door and the frame.

"They dusted for prints," Conner said. He opened the door and she followed him inside.

The porch was filled with plastic bags and newspapers. Conner went to the door of the trailer and turned the doorknob. It was locked. He took something out of his pocket and used it to open the door.

"You jimmied the lock!" Mel cried.

"Say it a little louder, why don't you?" he said.

"Sorry," she whispered.

They went up the two steps leading into the home and paused. The sun was setting, and inside, the place was dark. Conner pulled out a penlight from his pocket and turned it on.

"What are we looking for?" Mel asked.

"I'm not sure. Just wanted to look around."

He put the light on the floor in front of him. He took a few steps in and stopped. There was an outline on the floor, and a bloody stain on the carpet.

"He was hit on the head," Conner said.

"No kidding," she said.

He ran the light around the room. Jason Frye had died in his living room. Conner was looking for more blood. He found some on the corner of the built-in desk.

"There's blood on the corner. He hit his head. Maybe he was dizzy and hit the corner going down. That may be why I never heard about this. They might have ruled it an accident."

"Can we find out?"

"We can check with the locals to see what happened."

"What are you doing here?"

Mel jumped and turned around. In the doorway was the silhouette of a man.

"I'm a police officer," Conner said. "I'm investigating Mr. Frye's death."

"They already did that," the man said.

"What do you know about it, sir?" Conner asked.

"Come outta there and I'll tell you. You ain't gonna find anything in there anyway."

The man left the doorway and stood in the porch. Mel went out first, followed by Conner. The man was older, probably in his early seventies. He had a lit cigarette in his hand.

"What's your name, sir?" Conner asked.

"I'm Joe. I live next door."

"Did you know Mr. Frye?"

"Yeah, I knew him. Why don't we go to my house and sit down."

Mel didn't want to go into the guy's house, but Conner was following him. She thought about going back to the car, but she stayed near Conner. The guy had a porch, too, only there were lawn chairs in his. They all sat.

"I complained to the manager about the smell," Joe said. "It was pretty bad."

"Do you remember when that was?" Conner asked.

"Sometime near the end of September, I think.

"Did he have any visitors?"

"Nah. Jason was a prick. He didn't have any friends. Only his kid would show up now and then."

"Did he visit often?"

"I guess. He used to come here in a big car."

"What color was it?" Mel asked.

"Red I think. That dark red. They've got a name for it."

"Burgundy," Mel said.

"Yeah," Joe said. "Burgundy."

"When was the last time you saw him here?" Conner asked.

"Geez, it was a while. Maybe during the summer. He had some kind of thing going in Largo."

"What kind of thing?" Conner asked.

"Some old lady. The kid worked for a water company. Jason told me about it. The kid would deliver her water and she asked him to live with her."

"Why would she do that?" Mel asked.

"The kid was okay. He wasn't like his old man. I guess the old lady needed help and she liked the kid."

"But why would she ask him to live with her?" Mel asked.

"Who knows? Jason told me that she liked the kid. She had a spare room and offered it to the kid so he could help her out, you know, run errands and drive for her, stuff like that."

Joe took a drag off his cigarette. Conner could tell he

wanted to say something else, but he was stalling. Conner was just about to ask Joe what was on his mind when he began to talk again.

"These places," he waved his hand around, "you can hear every word. One night they were arguing. The old man wanted to run a con on the woman. He told her that if she sold her house to him, junior would work for her for nothin'."

"He wanted the woman to sign over her house in exchange for services?" Conner asked.

"Yeah. The kid didn't want to, though. That's why they argued."

Joe paused. He took a few drags off his cigarette.

"The old man drank. He was always three sheets to the wind. He bragged about his plan. He thought he was some criminal mastermind. Only I guess the lady wasn't buyin' it. She told him no." Joe took another drag from his cigarette. He coughed for about a minute, then took a deep breath. "She told the kid to get out. I heard Jason yellin' at the kid one night. The kid said she told him to leave."

"Did you tell the police about this?" Conner asked.

"No." Joe crushed his cigarette in the ashtray on the floor next to his chair. "It wasn't my business."

"But it's relevant," Conner said.

"I didn't want to rat on him. He was dead. What was the point?"

"But his son might have killed him."

"He didn't die that night. The night he died, the kid wasn't around. No red car. Oh, burgundy car. Besides, I'd have heard them fighting. Jason was drunk and fell. He hit his head. End of story."

"Shit," Conner said quietly. "Is there anything else you haven't told the police?"

Joe shook his head. He reached into his pocket and took out another cigarette. As he lit it, Conner stood.

"What's your last name?" Conner asked.

"Why do you need that?" Joe said.

"Your last name?"

"Welsh."

"Thanks."

Conner began to move and Mel got up and followed. They walked back to the car and when they got there, Conner made notes on the conversation they'd had with Joe Welsh. He noted the house numbers, too.

"What do you think?" Mel asked.

"I think he fell and hit his head. If the kid had been there, Joe would have told the police."

Mel felt her body shaking. "This pisses me off so much."

"What? That they planned it?"

"That she, shit. If she needed help, why didn't she call us? She and my grandmother were getting along. We could have done something for her."

"She didn't want to bother you. You live a thousand miles away. It might have seemed like an easy solution to her. And the kid might have been a con artist like his old man, only sober and charming."

It was getting dark. It was also dinnertime, and Conner's stomach was growling.

"You want to get something to eat?

———

MEL CALLED VERA AND TOLD HER SHE WOULD BE HOME BY nine. Vera told her she would wait up. Conner took her to Chili's.

Chili's was decorated for the holidays, too. Mel tried to

ignore them as the hostess sat them in a booth by the bar. After they ordered, Conner looked at Mel.

"So what do you do in New Jersey?"

"I manage a Starbucks. My supervisor made me take a vacation."

"They made you take a vacation?"

"Yeah. I guess three years is a long time to go without some time off. It's hard to take time off in that business."

"So this is your vacation."

"Yup, and I hadn't planned on coming here. My grandmother paid for my ticket."

"She's Audrey's sister?"

"Yes. I call her Nana Grace because she's my great-grandmother."

"It was nice of her to pay your fare here."

"She did it because she wanted me to check on Audrey." The server brought their drinks. "The truth is, I didn't have any plans, so when she asked me to do this, I thought, what the hell?"

"And your friend is staying down here."

"Lisa. Yes. Her dad owns a time share on Clearwater Beach. She asks me every year. This is the first time I've come close."

"Do you live alone?" he asked.

"Right now, yes."

"So do I."

Their food came and they ate in silence for a while. Mel studied Conner's face. His eyes were set apart by a perfectly shaped nose. He looked like one of those models in GQ.

"Why did you become a cop?" she asked. "You don't look like one."

"I always wanted to be one. I like putting the bad guys in jail."

"What if they aren't guilty?"

"That's what the system is for. The state attorney's office."

"I hope you can get this guy."

"That's why I'm taking my time."

They both ate too much and left the restaurant. He drove her back to her car.

"I have to work tomorrow," he said. "I can check out Jason Frye Sr. in the computer. Maybe I can talk to the investigating officer."

"You still don't have enough to take this to your supervisor, do you?"

"If the kid had killed the old man, or if we suspected he had, maybe. That's why I have to talk to the cops who did the invest."

"I'm gonna try to see my friend again tomorrow, but I'll have my phone with me."

"If I find out anything, I'll call."

He watched her get out of the car and into hers. She looked sad. He wanted to help her. He wanted to find out what had happened to her aunt, but he still didn't believe the outcome would be good.

Chapter Eleven

MEL WOKE UP WITH THE CAT ON HER HEAD. HE WAS purring and kneading her. She pushed him off and turned over onto her back. Vera wasn't up yet, but the sun was shining in the front window. Mel's phone was charging on the table next to the sofa. She reached for it, disconnected it, and turned it on. It was seven.

There was a message from Lisa and one from her grandmother. She listened to them. Lisa was sorry, but she had met a hot guy and had been distracted. She promised it wouldn't happen again if Mel wanted to come to the beach. Her grandmother said she would be home if Mel needed to call.

Mel didn't feel like going to the beach. She wanted to go back to Audrey's neighborhood and talk to the people living on her street. She wasn't sure it would do any good, but she had to do something. The not knowing was killing her.

She heard Vera open her bedroom door. The cat ran to the hallway. Soon, she saw Vera hobbling into the kitchen. Vera saw Mel was awake.

"Good morning," she said.

"Morning," Mel said.

"Would you like coffee this morning?" Vera asked.

"Please," Mel said.

"I'm almost out. I have to go to the store."

"I can take you," Mel said.

"You're sure you don't mind?" Vera asked.

"Not at all."

"That would be very nice. It would save me paying for a taxi." Vera filled the coffeemaker and took some things out of the fridge. "Have you found out anything more about Audrey?"

"Not really. We still don't know where she is."

"Did you spend the whole day with the policeman?"

"Yup." Mel sat up and put her feet on the floor. "We found out that the kid living there had forged his name on the title to her home."

"Well, that's something. Can't they arrest him for that?"

"Conner, the policeman, said it's not enough to arrest him for. We have to have more of a case."

"Well, I guess he knows what he's doing. What would you like for breakfast?"

"Do you have some cereal?" Mel asked.

"I have bran flakes."

Mel made a face. It was not what she had in mind. "Do you have bread? I could have some toast."

"I have a nice multigrain bread."

"That's good."

Vera took the bread out of the freezer and stuck two slices in the toaster. The coffeemaker was perking and the smell filled the little home. Mel got up and went to the bathroom. When she came out, she was dressed and sat at the table where Vera had placed her toast.

Vera brought two cups of coffee to the table and sat across from Mel. "We can go after I get dressed."

Mel nodded as she buttered her toast. "Where do you usually go?"

"I like Publix. The one right over there," she pointed out the window, "is very clean."

"Then Publix it is."

It didn't take Vera long to dress and they were in Publix by nine. Vera used a scooter to navigate the large store while Mel looked around on her own with a cart. She put some things in the cart and then stopped dead in her tracks. Jason was in the aisle, but he hadn't seen her yet.

She watched him as he put things in his cart. She backed away. He was a good-looking guy, and she believed he could have fooled an old, lonely woman. She got to the end of the aisle and moved in front of it. She peeked around the corner so she could still see him. Vera came up behind her.

"Are you playing hide and seek?" she asked.

Mel jumped, then turned to see Vera. "No. I just saw that guy who is in my aunt's home."

"Really? Where is he?" Vera road past her and looked down the aisle. "Is that him?"

"Yes, but be quiet. I don't want him to see me."

"He looks like that boy on TV. The good-looking one. What's his name again? He's on something at night."

"We'll figure it out later," Mel said. "Are you ready to check out?"

"I think so."

They went to the checkout and Mel insisted on paying for Vera's items. Vera protested, but not too much, before letting Mel pay.

Vera rode the scooter to the car and Mel put the bags in the trunk. She saw Jason come out of the store and get into the Mercury. She helped Vera into her car and got in the driver's side.

She followed the Mercury out the side of the parking lot. She saw it turn into a bank. There was nowhere for her to park so she just kept going. She wished she didn't have Vera with her for she wanted to go to Audrey's while he was out and look around.

Once she got Vera squared away, Mel got back into her car and drove over to Audrey's park. Something was up. There was a sheriff's car parked in front of Marge's house.

Mel parked in back of it and got out of her car. Marge was in tears and another woman had her arm around her. The deputy was taking notes. It wasn't Conner. Mel glanced at Audrey's home and didn't see the Mercury. She wanted to find out what had happened to Marge, but she couldn't pass up the chance to check out Audrey's place while Jason was out. She decided to take a walk between Audrey's home and the one next door. If anyone asked, she could say she was going to the pool.

The home's foundation consisted of staggered cement blocks. The driveway ran up the right side, and next to it was a strip of dirt where Audrey had planted bushes. There was also a strip of dirt that ran along the back of the house. The central air conditioner was on the left side.

Mel walked to the back of the house. She looked at the bushes as she walked by them. She had no idea what she was looking for, but it felt like she was doing something. When she got to the back of the house, she noticed something strange. Audrey hadn't planted anything there. Some of the dirt in the strip behind the house was darker than the rest. Someone had been digging there.

She heard a car coming into the driveway. She hid behind the home and waited until she heard a car door open and close. Then she waited until she heard the door to the home open and close before walking along the left side of the house. He would be in the kitchen and wouldn't see her.

She ran to the front of the home and across the street. The deputy was getting into his car and the woman with Marge was walking with her back to Marge's house. Mel followed them.

"What happened?" she called after them.

The woman turned and looked at Mel. "Her dog is missing."

"Maurice?" Mel asked.

"Yes."

Mel reached them as they neared the door. "When did this happen?"

"Wait a minute," the woman said. She opened the door and helped Marge get inside. "I'll tell you in a minute."

Mel waited ten minutes for the woman. She came out and was shaking her head.

"This will be the death of her," the woman said.

"I'm Mel. My aunt lives across the street."

"I'm Sharon. I'm her sister."

"What happened to Maurice?"

"She was in the bathroom when he got out. She found the sliding door open when she got out and he was gone. She called and he didn't come."

"And she called the police?"

"She wanted to report him stolen. She can't imagine him just wandering off."

"But you think he did just wander off."

"Maurice wasn't the most obedient dog. He didn't come when she called. I bet he's somewhere down the street. I'm gonna ride around and see if I can find him."

All of a sudden, Mel thought of the dirt in back of Audrey's home.

"That's a good idea," she said. "Nice to meet you, Sharon."

Mel got back into her car. She opened the windows. She wasn't sure what to do. She had a gut feeling, but she dismissed it. It was too horrible to think about. She decided to wait and see if Jason went out again.

Chapter Twelve

MEL WAS CHECKING HER FACEBOOK PAGE WHEN SHE HEARD a car start. She saw the Mercury backing up and lay down on her seat. When she heard it drive away, she sat up and got out of the car.

She ran across the street and to the back yard. She looked around for something to dig with, then thought of the shed at the back of the driveway. She went to the shed and stepped inside. There was a rack of gardening tools over a sink. She grabbed the trowel and went back outside.

The old man next door, the one who had talked to Mel the first day she came looking for Audrey, was standing in his driveway and gave her a dirty look.

"What are you doing in there?"

"None of your business," she said, and continued on to the back yard.

She stuck the trowel in the darker dirt and began to dig. It wasn't long before she saw one of Maurice's legs.

"Shit," she said. The old man was standing nearby.

"Oh, my God," he said.

"Shhh," Mel said. "Do you want to kill Marge?" He put his hand over his mouth. "Go and call the police."

"Why don't you call the police?" he asked.

"Because I'm trespassing and will be arrested. You can say you saw something funny. Tell them you think your neighbor killed Maurice. That ought to get them out here."

She covered Maurice's leg and wiped her prints off the trowel. She also wiped off the handle on the door, then went to her car.

She wanted to call Conner. She wanted to tell him Jason had killed Maurice, but she still wasn't sure why he had done it. She remembered Marge telling her that Maurice had been barking for the last three months. Conner thought he might be smelling something.

She turned on the car and drove away. She didn't want the cops to see her parked there. With nowhere else to go, she called Lisa. It was ten and the call went to voicemail.

She left a message and hung up the phone. She thought about her aunt. In her heart, she knew they wouldn't find her alive, but she still couldn't entertain that thought. She kept pushing it aside, trying to keep the belief that she had taken a cruise. It was easier to keep going that way.

She thought about the mall across the street from the mobile home park. Shopping always helped her relax. She drove to the mall. Every parking space was taken. Christmas shoppers. Mel's shoulders dropped. Christmas was in three days. She was supposed to leave tomorrow, Friday. There was no way she could go until she knew what had happened to Audrey.

She rode around until she found an empty spot near Target and parked. She hoped Lisa would call her back soon and left her phone on.

As Mel shopped at Target, Conner was sitting in the Clearwater Police Department reading the case file for Jason Frye Sr. The detective had concluded that the death was an accident and the case was closed. Conner was disappointed. He'd hoped they had looked into Jason Jr.

When he got back to his car, he looked at his computer and found a message. The dispatcher was asking for an officer to go to Holiday Oaks mobile home park to respond to a 911 call from a resident. He saw that another officer had responded, but he wanted to see what was going on and headed that way.

He saw the patrol car sitting in front of Jason Jr.'s home and parked behind it. He walked to the door and was about to knock when he saw Ben Kiernan, another deputy, coming around from the back of the home.

"Hey," Conner said.

Ben nodded. "Maurice is dead."

"What?" Conner asked.

"Maurice, the dog, is dead. He was buried behind this place. A neighbor called it in."

"When did this happen?"

"Right after you spoke to the woman across the street."

"When?" Conner asked.

"Today," Ben said.

"I didn't talk to her today."

"Oh, I thought you were the one who took the report. The lady across the street called in a dognapping. Then this guy," the deputy pointed at the old man's house with his thumb, "called in and said he thought Maurice was dead. Well, he was right."

"Someone killed the dog."

"That's what it looks like."

The Mercury wasn't parked in the driveway. "This guy did it."

"You know who lives here?" the deputy asked.

"Yup. I was here two days ago."

"I called animal control. They're gonna pick Maurice up and find the cause of death. If he killed the dog, we may be looking at animal cruelty."

"Why would he kill the dog?" Conner asked.

"Who knows? Some whack job who doesn't like animals. Or he had it in for the lady across the street."

The deputy left Conner and went back to his cruiser. Conner walked around to the back of the house and looked at Maurice. The dog was covered in dirt. There was no way to tell what he had been doing before he met his demise.

Conner walked around the house and looked at the ground. Maybe the dog was digging and Jason caught him. Conner didn't see any signs of digging on the left side of the home. He went to the front. There was a planter made of stacked stones cemented in place. It went the length of the front of the house. Conner looked at the stones. Toward the middle, he saw white marks on one of the stones. They looked like scratch marks.

Conner went to the shed. He took the same trowel that Mel had used and came back to the front of the house. He began to dig the dirt out of the planter. He dug all the way to the bottom and didn't find anything. If a body had been buried there, he would have found it.

He moved the dirt around to cover the hole. He didn't want Jason to know what he had seen. He put the trowel back. His hands were muddy. He tried turning on the sink in the shed, but it was dry.

He went back to his cruiser and took out a container of

wipes from the glove box. He cleaned his hands as best he could. He was frustrated. The dog had been killed, but why? It had known something. It had smelled something, but the planter was empty. It was time to talk to his supervisor about investigating Jason Frye Jr.

Chapter Thirteen

Mark Allen, Conner's supervisor, sat behind a big, gray metal desk. Files filled one side. He kept rubbing his face. Conner was pressing him hard for a warrant, and Mark was trying to find some way to dissuade him. There just wasn't enough proof that Jason had hurt a human being.

"He killed a dog; that's probable cause," Conner said.

"It's animal cruelty, not murder."

"But the lady is missing, and the dog knew something."

"Conner, I admire your tenacity, but you don't have a case here."

"The kid forged her name on the title to her home."

"So, we charge him with forgery. But we can't, because you didn't have a warrant."

Conner was fuming. He knew Jason Jr. had done something to Audrey Glenn. But there was no body or proof that a murder had taken place.

"There is something you could check on," Mark said. "He's gonna be charged with animal cruelty. Talk to the state attorney about subpoenaing his bank records."

Conner smiled. "To check his income."

"If he offed the old lady, he probably didn't tell Social Security."

"And that would involve the feds."

"At least you'd have probable cause to investigate. He'd have to produce Audrey Glenn."

"Okay. I'll talk to the state attorney."

Conner would have to wait until Jason was charged before talking to them. Then he'd have to wait until he found out who'd been assigned the case. Animal Cruelty was a third-degree felony, but Jason might only be fined and given probation, not jailed. Conner wanted to pin his ass to the wall.

He got into his cruiser. He was assigned to patrol Clearwater and so far, he'd spent most of his time investigating Audrey's disappearance. He had to spend some time on the road.

His phone rang. It was Mel.

"Hey," he said.

"Did you get a call about Maurice?"

"Yeah. How did you know about that?"

"I found him. I had the old guy next door call you."

"Why didn't you call?"

"I was afraid I'd get arrested for trespassing."

Conner laughed. "Wouldn't that be something?"

"Did Jason do it?" she asked.

"I'm sure he did, but animal control has to find out what killed him."

"Did anyone tell Marge?"

Shit, Conner thought. "I don't know. I didn't see Ben go to her house. Maybe he figured I'd go and tell her."

"Can we go talk to Marge?"

"Do you really think she'll want to talk?"

"I would if someone killed my dog. I'd want to tell the world who did it."

"Would she think it was Jason?"

She was quiet for a few seconds. "I don't know. I guess I would because of what we know about him."

"We don't know enough about him," Conner said. "What did Joe say last night? Something about Jason delivering water. I wonder where he worked."

"How many water companies are there that deliver water here?"

"Not many. Shouldn't be too hard to find. But I really have to work today. I'm supposed to be in Clearwater."

"I can go see Marge alone."

"You've got to ask her how Maurice got out alone."

"Okay. Anything else?"

"If she knows of anyone who would want to hurt Maurice."

"I can do that. Are you off later on?"

"At seven. Do you want to meet for dinner?"

Her heart began to beat faster. She'd love to, but she hadn't seen Lisa yet. "I was going to my friend's place today. I'll probably go out with her later."

"Oh." Was that disappointment she heard? "Well, I'll call you if I learn anything."

"Thanks, Conner."

After she hung up the phone, she fought the urge to call him back and say she would see him for dinner. She really had to visit Lisa. She went to her car and drove back to the park. The Mercury was there. She wondered why the cops hadn't come to arrest him.

She walked up the driveway of Marge's home and knocked on the side door. Sharon answered.

"May I speak to Marge?" Mel asked.

"Sure, honey, come in."

"I need to tell you something," Mel said softly. "They found Maurice's body buried across the street."

Sharon's eyes widened and her mouth dropped open.

"Who would do that?" she whispered.

"It's being investigated. I just wanted to ask Marge if she knew of anyone who would want to hurt him."

"We have to tell her. Oh, she'll fall apart."

"Maybe if we do it together it won't be so bad."

Sharon went to the living room and Mel followed. Marge was sitting in a recliner. She looked at Mel and narrowed her eyes.

"Do I know you?" she asked.

"I was here the other day. I'm Audrey's niece."

"That's right. I remember."

"Marge," Sharon said. "We have something to tell you."

Marge moved the handle on the recliner and put her feet down.

"Marge, they found Maurice."

"Where is he?" Marge asked.

"He's dead, Marge," Sharon said.

Marge's face drained of color. She began to shake. "Oh, my God."

"The police are looking into it," Mel said. "Do you know of anyone who would want to hurt him?"

"Of course not," Marge said. "Why would anyone want to hurt…oh, Maurice."

Marge began to cry. Sharon went to her and put her arm around Marge's shoulders.

"He was found behind Audrey's home," Mel said.

Now Marge looked angry. "That son of a bitch."

"Who, Marge?" Sharon asked.

"That kid that lives there. He was always yelling at me to shut Maurice up. He hated Maurice."

"Marge," Mel said, "how did Maurice get out of the house?"

Marge started crying again. "It was my fault. I must have left the sliding door open when I went to the bathroom. He would have been able to slip through the rail and jump down."

"When was the last time you saw Maurice?" Mel asked.

"This morning. We were up early. It was still dark. Oh, Maurice."

"I'm sorry," Sharon said. She turned to Mel. "I think you should go now."

Mel nodded. "Thank you, and I'm so sorry for your loss."

Mel left the home and walked down the driveway to her car. Jason was standing across the street with a cigarette in his hand. He looked at her and she felt a chill run up her spine. He kept staring as she got into the car. He was still staring when she drove away.

Chapter Fourteen

THE RADIO PLAYED NOTHING BUT CHRISTMAS SONGS. MEL wished she could plug her phone into the radio so she could listen to her own music, but the economy model only came with a radio and CD player. Who listened to CD's anymore?

The Christmas decorations were getting to her. Everywhere she went there was some reminder of the season. Mel's Christmases hadn't been very uplifting. They were usually spent with her grandmother, who tried to make up for Linda's neglect.

Mel thought about her mother as she drove to Clearwater Beach. She hadn't heard from her in over a year. Laura tried to make light of it by saying Linda was busy, that her job took up all of her time, but Mel knew the truth. Linda just didn't care.

She turned off the causeway and onto the road leading to Lisa's condo. When she got there, she found a spot nearby and parked. It had a meter. She would have to see if there was a place to park that came with the condo. She dialed her number. This time, Lisa picked up.

"Where are you?" she asked.

"I'm outside the condo."

"I'll be right down."

Lisa was in a bathing suit. She smiled when she saw Mel.

"Damn, how long has it been?" Lisa asked.

"At least a year."

"Well, you look good." Lisa noticed the parking meter. "You can park under the condo."

Lisa pointed to a driveway leading under the building.

"Aren't you using it?" Mel said.

"There are two spots for each unit."

They got into Mel's car and Lisa showed her where the parking spots were, then took Mel up to the condo. It was on the second floor of a four-unit building. Two condos were on top, and two were on the bottom.

"Dad couldn't come this year," Lisa said.

"Doesn't he mind you missing Christmas?" Mel asked.

"He's in Barcelona. He won't be back until after the new year."

Lisa's mom had passed away two years before from breast cancer. Lisa wouldn't talk about her mother to anyone but Mel.

"So," Lisa asked, "how long are you here for?"

"I'm supposed to leave tomorrow, but I still don't know what happened to my aunt."

"Did you talk to the cops?"

"There's this cop who has been helping me, kind of on the sly. Not officially."

"Is he young?" Lisa asked with a smile.

"He is. He's cute, too."

"Really? What's his name?"

"Conner O'Keefe."

"Conner is a nice name."

Sandy walked in. She was a friend of Lisa's from work. She had her suitcase in her hand.

"Sandy, this is Mel."

"Hi," Sandy said. "My taxi should be here soon."

"Sandy has to go home for Christmas," Lisa said. Sandy didn't look happy about it.

"I wish I didn't have to go at all," Sandy said. "The whole family is going to be there. All the of them. It's gonna be a nightmare."

Mel wished she could have such a nightmare. "Sorry."

"She'll get over it," Lisa said. "Anyway, do you have your bathing suit?"

"Yeah. I got one at Target."

Mel pulled the two-piece suit out of her bag.

"Did you steal it?" Lisa asked.

"NO! I put it in there after I paid for it."

"Good. I didn't want to have to bail you out of jail."

They heard a horn beep and Sandy picked up her bag.

"Well, it's nice meeting you," she said to Mel, then turned to Lisa. "I'll call you when I get home."

Lisa went to her and hugged her. "It will all work out."

"Yeah, I know."

After Sandy left, Lisa grabbed a towel. "Hurry up and change."

Mel went to the bathroom and put on her suit.

"Do you have an extra towel?" she asked.

"In the closet in the bathroom."

She found one and went to the living room. Lisa was looking at her phone.

"Do you have another pair of flip-flops?" Mel asked.

"In the bedroom. Hurry up."

Mel ran to the bedroom and put on the pair of flip-flops near the closet. She also grabbed a bottle of sunblock off the dresser. When she went back to Lisa, they left the condo and walked to the beach. Mel forgot to take her phone.

———————

THE CASSIDY WATER COMPANY WAS LOCATED IN NORTH Clearwater. Conner parked in the main parking lot and went to the front entrance. The receptionist smiled when he walked inside. He was in uniform.

"Hi," he said. "I need to talk to someone from human resources."

"That would be Jolene," the woman said. "I'll see if she's available."

Jolene came through a door adjacent to the receptionist and smiled.

"How can I help you, Officer?"

"I need to check the work schedule of one of your employees."

"Come on back," she said, and Conner followed her. She took him to her office. She sat behind the desk while he sat in a seat in front of it. "What's the employee's name?"

"Jason Frye. I don't know if he's still working here."

"I remember Jason. Blue eyes. He liked to flirt." She typed something into the computer. "He left us in September."

"Why?"

"He quit. He didn't give a reason."

"What was the date?"

"September 15. He worked out the week."

"Did you ever talk to him?"

"What do you mean?"

"Other than about work."

"No. He didn't talk to me about his personal life."

"Was he friends with anyone?"

"Why do you want to know?" she asked.

"I'm investigating him."

Jolene sat back in her chair. "I think he was dating one of the women who work in the warehouse. Susan. Susan Blaine."

"Is she working today?"

"Yes. The warehouse works Monday through Friday."

"Can I go back there?"

"I can call her to come here." Jolene got on the phone and spoke to someone in the warehouse. "Thanks," she said. She looked at Conner. "She's coming. The office next door is empty if you want privacy."

"Thanks," Conner said.

Ten minutes later, a young woman with long brown hair tied back in a ponytail appeared at Jolene's door.

"Susan, this is Officer...I'm sorry. I didn't catch your name."

"Deputy O'Keefe," Conner said.

"The deputy would like to speak to you about Jason Frye."

Susan's face hardened. "I don't know what I can tell you."

"Take the deputy to the office next door," Jolene said.

Susan led Conner to the empty office and he shut the door.

"Jason is under investigation."

"That doesn't surprise me," she said. "He has shit for brains."

"How well do you know him?" Conner asked.

"We went out for like six months. He was all right."

"He was all right?"

"He was a nice guy, but he liked to scam people. He tried it with me. That's when I dumped him."

Conner wasn't convinced Susan had dumped Jason.

"What kind of people did he like to scam?"

Susan leaned against the desk. "Old people. Old ladies. He'd turn on the charm and they'd tip him well."

"That doesn't sound like a scam."

"One of them asked him to live with her. He told me he got her to sign over her car to him. He showed up here one day in this huge old car."

"Is that all?"

Susan looked at her hands. "He told me his father had asked him to help him with something bigger. I didn't like his father."

"Why?"

"Because he was always drunk and would hit on me whenever he was around me. I got sick of it."

"What was the something bigger?"

Susan shuffled her feet. "I really don't know for sure. He told me some of it, but it seemed more like he was helping his father than doing it himself."

"It was what?"

Susan sighed. "The old man wanted this woman's house. He wanted Jason to help him get it. Jason wasn't that smart, you know? He was cute and women liked him, but he did such stupid things."

"For instance."

"For instance he drove his old car into that water at the dog beach. It got stuck and had to be junked. He was an idiot."

"That beach off the causeway?"

"Yeah. I had a dog and we took her there. She...was a good dog."

"Was?"

"She got hit by a car." Susan started to cry.

"I'm sorry to hear that. You haven't asked me why I'm

investigating him."

"Why are you?"

"He killed a dog."

"That son of a bitch."

She wrapped her arms around herself.

"Susan, do you know anything about that woman he was trying to scam, the one with the house?"

"All I know is that Jason didn't want to do it. He was stupid for sure, but he liked the woman. For some reason, he didn't want to take advantage of her."

Conner thought about something she had said. "What scam did he try on you?"

"I inherited five hundred bucks from my grandmother. He wanted me to give it to him so he could invest it in something. He wouldn't tell me exactly what. Said he wanted me to trust him. I was kind of over him by then so I just told him to get lost."

"Have you spoken to him since?"

"No."

Again, Conner wasn't convinced she hadn't spoken to Jason.

"Does he have any other friends?"

"No. He's kind of a loner. He doesn't get along with guys that well."

Susan was looking at the ground. She was still holding herself.

"Thanks," Conner said. "We're done."

"Will he go to jail?"

"Probably not, unless the judge is an animal lover. Then he'll probably get thirty days."

"That sucks. He should go away longer for killing a dog."

"Agreed."

Conner got into his cruiser. He pulled up Jason Frye to

see if he had been arrested. He had been picked up fifteen minutes ago and was being taken to the Pinellas County Jail for booking.

Conner drove to the State Attorney's Office in Clearwater. He was looking for Sam Cannon, the son of the current state attorney. Sam was an assistant state attorney and had been assigned Jason Frye's case. Conner wanted to see if an animal cruelty charge would give Sam a reason to get hold of Audrey's bank statements.

Sam's office was on the third floor of the criminal justice center. His secretary smiled when Conner walked in.

"Deputy," she said.

"Ma'am," Conner said. "Is Mr. Cannon in?"

"I'll see if he has a minute," she said. She got up and went to the door behind her. She went inside and when she came out, she waved to Conner.

"He'll see you."

The office wasn't that impressive. Sam Cannon wasn't very neat. There were files everywhere and when Conner walked in, Sam had his feet propped up on the desk.

"Deputy," he said.

"Mr. Cannon."

"Sit."

Conner sat in the folding chair set in front of Sam's desk.

"What can I do for you, Deputy?"

"You know that case you just got, the one with the dog killer?"

"What's the name?"

"Jason Frye."

"I haven't really looked at the file yet. He's on the docket for tomorrow. What about him?"

"I'm working a missing persons. The person is missing

from the mobile home he's living in."

Sam's eyebrows went up. He put his feet down and sat forward in his chair. He put his arms out and clasped his hands.

"And you suspect what?"

"Off the record?"

"Off the record."

"I think he might have killed an old woman."

"That's interesting. Why do you think he killed an old woman?"

"He killed the dog. The dog had been barking since the old woman disappeared. Something's just not right. I don't have anything to go on but my gut. I need some hard evidence."

"Like?"

"Like her bank statements."

"I assume you've been to the house."

"I spoke to the guy. I asked where she was and he claims she went on a cruise to Europe."

"What makes you think she didn't?"

"She's ninety and she doesn't have a passport."

"Do you know that for sure?"

"As sure as I'm gonna be for now."

"This isn't enough to support a subpoena. You said you were working a missing persons case. Who filed it?"

"Her niece."

"Does the niece have a power of attorney?"

"I don't know."

"If she does, she can go to the bank and ask them directly. It would be faster."

"So you won't do it?"

"Try getting them with the niece first."

"Okay. But if we can't, I'll be back."

"Come back with more."

Chapter Fifteen

IT WAS GETTING DARK WHEN THE GIRLS GOT BACK TO THE condo. Lisa was in a New York frame of mind. Dark equaled cold. Being in Florida in December took some getting used to. She handed Mel her towel and phone while she fiddled with the lock on the condo door.

"I keep forgetting to leave this light on," she said about the porch light. "And that it gets dark by five o'clock."

"Vera will be eating her dinner now," Mel said.

"Is that the old lady you're staying with?"

"Yeah. She's nice. She stays out of my business."

"That's good. Shit. I can't get this key to go in."

"I forgot my phone. Does your phone have a flashlight?"

"Yeah." Lisa took the phone from her bag and scrolled through her apps. She found the flashlight and turned it on. "There you are."

She put the key into the lock, opened the door, and turned on the kitchen light.

"I should just leave that outside light on all the time," Lisa said.

"Would they get pissed if you did?"

"No. This is a private place. No one is watching."

"Is there any food here?" Mel asked.

"No. Sandy and I ate out all the time. You hungry already?"

Mel's stomach was on Vera time. "Yeah, kind of."

"I guess we could go eat. We have to change. By then it will be six. But the clubs don't get going until nine or ten. What will we do for four hours?"

"We're going to clubs?" Mel asked. She had to call Vera and tell her she wouldn't be coming there.

"What did you think? Come on, Mel. This is why we're here."

"Um, okay. I've gotta make a phone call."

Mel went to Sandy's vacated bedroom and closed the door. She really didn't feel like going to clubs. She usually got up at five for work. Her body had grown so used to getting up early and going to bed early that the thought of going out after eight made her anxious.

Mel was tired. Her neck hurt. She was still worried about Audrey and wondered if Conner had learned anything new. She also wanted to see him. She missed him, but she didn't want to talk to Lisa about him. She wanted to keep it to herself for a while longer until she was sure there was something to talk about.

She tried to think of some excuse to get out of staying in the condo for the night. Lisa would never believe Mel was worried about Vera. Maybe she could say her grandmother called and wanted her to come home. Lisa might buy that. Then she felt bad about wanting to ditch her friend. What was wrong with her? She and Lisa had always gone out together, and Lisa would always drink too much. It didn't bother Mel when they were eighteen, but at twenty-six, she didn't feel like holding her friend's hair out of the toilet while she puked.

She noticed a message from Conner. As she listened to the message, she thought about what a nice voice he had. He said he had talked to animal control and their vet confirmed that Maurice had died from blunt force trauma to his head. That meant someone bashed the poor dog over the head and killed him. Since the dog was buried behind Audrey's house, that made Jason Jr. the likely suspect.

He'd been picked up and taken to the county jail. Conner also asked if Audrey had given anyone her power of attorney. That was at three. She called him back and got his voicemail.

"Hey, sorry I missed your call. I was at the beach with a friend and forgot my phone." She looked at the time. It was twenty after five. "Listen, if you get this message before six, call me."

She hung up. She hoped he would call. She could then tell Lisa she had to leave. But that wouldn't stop Lisa from going out alone. She was fearless. Shit. Mel would have to stay. Before she went back to Lisa, she called Laura.

"Hey, Grandma," she said.

"Hi, dear. How are things going?"

"I still haven't any news for you. I called to ask if you have a power of attorney for Audrey."

"I don't think so. She did send me a copy of her will a while back. Maybe there was one with that. I have to look for it. Why do you need to know that?"

"Just something the deputy asked for. I'm not sure why."

"Well, I'll look for it and let you know."

"How's Nana Grace doing?" Mel asked.

"She's worried. I'm trying to keep her occupied, but she keeps asking if you saw Audrey."

"Tell her I miss her. Tell her I got stuck at Lisa's and haven't had a chance to go back to the mobile home park but I promise I will before I come home."

"Do you think you'll be back by Christmas?"

"I don't know. I miss you. I want to be there for Christmas."

"Call me when you know. I miss you, too, Mel."

When Mel hung up, she felt sad. Nana Grace was worried. Mel was trying to spare her, but her imagination was probably worse than what Mel knew. She thought about what Conner had said, that Jason was in the county jail. That meant he wasn't home. The home was empty.

"Do you need something to wear?" Lisa asked when Mel emerged from the bedroom.

"Yeah. I have dresses, but I feel cold. I want something that will cover my legs."

"There's nothing wrong with your legs," Lisa said.

"No, it's not that. I'm just cold."

"Cold! You should be in New York right now. Come on, Mel! Once you start dancing, you'll warm up."

"Yeah, but before that, I'll freeze. Do you have something else?"

"I may have a pair of leggings, or you could wear tights."

"Let me see the leggings."

"They're in the second drawer."

Mel went to the dresser and looked in the middle drawer. She found a pair of black leggings. She went through the closet again and found a black, silk shell. The leggings were spandex and when she put them on, they hugged her butt.

Why didn't I think of these before? she thought.

When she emerged from the bedroom, Lisa made a face.

"You look like you're going to a funeral."

"I do not."

"We're supposed to be having fun, remember?"

"I'm not really in the mood for fun."

Lisa looked at Mel's face. "You don't want to go out tonight, do you?"

"Not really."

Mel's phone rang. She looked at the caller. "I've gotta take this." She went back into the bedroom and closed the door before answering. "Hello, Conner."

"How was the beach today?"

"We had a good time talking. I haven't seen her in a while."

"Did you get my message?"

"Yes. My grandmother is looking for a power of attorney."

"They picked up Jason. He's spending the night in jail."

"That means my aunt's house is empty."

"Mel, don't go getting any ideas. Legally, it's his house."

"We could look in the windows."

"Don't go near the home. Someone will see you, then I'll have to put you in a cell next to him."

"I wasn't planning on going alone."

"Did you think I would go with you?" Conner asked.

"He's under arrest. Can't you get a search warrant or something?"

"Not for animal abuse. The dog was found outside the home."

"Oh. So we can't get inside."

"No, and I better not catch you trying to."

"Okay." She paused. "What will happen to him?"

"He'll be arraigned and bail will be set."

"Will he go to jail?"

"I doubt it. He'll probably get probation and fines. Whatever the statutes allow. Or he could plead to a lesser charge."

"That sucks."

"Big ones." Conner paused. "Like I said, don't let me catch you near his home."

I wouldn't dream of it, she thought. "I'm going to a club with Lisa. I won't have time to snoop."

"A club? Which one?" he asked.

"I have no idea. Lisa's in charge of that."

"Be careful. The beach is full of idiots this time of year."

"We can take care of ourselves."

"Yeah, but still, be careful. Don't drink and drive. The patrols are out in force right now and you will get picked up."

"I promise. Cross my heart."

"Will you be in Largo tomorrow?" he asked.

"Why?"

"I'm off. I thought we could have lunch."

She felt a tingle rise up in her stomach. "I can be there. What time?"

"Well, if you're going out tonight, why don't we make it for two."

"Where should I meet you?"

"In the sheriff's parking lot. Like before."

"I'll be there."

She hung up and held the phone to her chest. She had to admit she liked him. She also had to admit that her aunt's home was calling her name.

Mel called Vera and told her she wouldn't be staying

with her that night, and Vera sounded disappointed. Mel told her she would stop by for a visit before she left Florida and that seemed to appease Vera.

She left the bedroom and found Lisa sitting at the kitchen table fixing her makeup. She sat across from her and smiled.

"The guy who's in my aunt's home is in jail. The house is empty."

Lisa looked over her handheld mirror. "You have that look on your face."

"What look?"

"That 'Let's go see what's in my aunt's house,' look."

"It's dark. We could look around without anybody bothering us."

"And if the guy next door sees us and calls the cops?"

"The people around there go to bed early. We could park a block away and walk over. Come on, Lisa. Please go with me."

"Do you still want to get something to eat?"

"Well, yeah."

"So we'll go to your aunt's after we eat?"

"Yeah."

Lisa put the mirror down. "Can we go to a club when we're done snooping around?"

Mel smiled. "Absolutely."

Chapter Sixteen

CONNER CLOCKED OUT OF WORK AND HEADED HOME. HE kept thinking about Mel. He was glad she'd agreed to have lunch with him. When he drove home, he passed Holiday Oaks and thought of driving in. He wanted to check out the house, too, but knew the consequences if he were caught. He didn't want to screw up this investigation. If Jason Jr. had done something to Audrey Glenn, Conner wanted him to pay.

Conner lived in an apartment building a few miles from the sheriff's office. His one-bedroom unit was on the second floor. He liked the quiet. No one walking over his head.

He changed out of his uniform and into a T-shirt and jeans. He opened his refrigerator door and looked inside. Nothing appealed to him. He thought about calling Mel to see if she and her friend were eating out. He could join them. But she had already agreed to see him the next day. Would she feel like he was stalking her if he called again?

He sat on his sofa and turned on the TV. He scrolled through the channels and found nothing of interest.

This is stupid, he thought. He pulled out his phone and called Mel. It went to voicemail. Maybe she was in the shower, or maybe she just didn't feel like talking to him again and ignored the call.

He looked at the time. It was six-thirty. Jason Jr. came into his mind. That home was just sitting there – empty. He could open the lock as he had with Jason Sr.'s place. The people there had seen him before. They knew he was a deputy. Technically, though, it would be breaking and entering.

Shit, he thought, and grabbed his jacket off the kitchen chair. He made sure his apartment was locked before heading to his car.

———

THEY USED LISA'S CAR TO DRIVE TO LARGO. MEL DIDN'T want to use hers in case Conner drove through the park. Just thinking that made her feel guilty, but the need to know what was inside that house trumped her conscience.

"Where should I park?" Lisa asked.

They were two blocks from the home. "We can park in the parking lot by the pool. It's just up ahead."

Lisa pulled into a spot and they got out. She followed Mel to the pool area and past the clubhouse.

"It's really dark here," Lisa said.

"Just stay with me."

They came up behind one row of houses and walked between two to the street. A dog barked. They crossed the street and went between two more homes before getting to the back of Audrey's home. The Mercury was parked in the driveway.

"I think this is it," Mel said. "We have to go to the front to be sure."

Lisa was growing excited. "This is kind of fun."

"As long as we don't get caught."

"So old people live here?"

"Some are old, some are just like your father."

They walked past Audrey's. The streetlight in front of the home shone on metal numbers 298.

"This is it," Mel said.

"So how do we get in?"

Mel turned and went back up the driveway and stopped in a dark spot under the carport. "I'm not sure."

"I thought you had a key." Lisa said.

"Why would I have a key?"

"It's your aunt's house, right?"

"I don't have a key."

"So, what, you want to break in?"

"I was kind of hoping you'd know how."

"Why would you think that?" Lisa said.

"Because you break into your father's house all the time."

"That's different."

"How is it different?"

"I've got a pick for that lock. That doesn't mean it will work for just any door."

"Can you try?"

"It's too dark. If we shine a flashlight on it, we'll be seen."

"You're gonna be seen anyway, ladies." A light flashed onto their faces. Mel recognized Conner's voice. "You just had to come here."

He turned off the light and came over to them. Mel could see he was not in uniform.

"So did you," she said.

"That's different," he said.

"How is that different? You're not in uniform."

"Yeah, but, well, it's just different."

"Who is this guy?" Lisa asked.

"He's a cop investigating my aunt's disappearance."

"Unofficially," Conner said.

"Yeah, unofficially," Mel said.

"So, are you gonna arrest us?" Lisa asked.

"He's not gonna arrest us," Mel said. "Are you?"

"I could take you in for trespassing. But since I'm here unofficially, no, I'm not gonna arrest you."

"Can you get inside?" Mel asked.

"I think so. Keep an eye out for me."

He went to the side door and shined his light on it. He turned off the light and took his picks out of his pocket. He managed to get them inside the keyhole and felt for the tumbler. When he got the door opened, he smiled.

"If we go in, nobody touches anything or moves anything."

Mel and Lisa nodded, but it was too dark to see.

"Did you hear me?" he asked.

"Yes, we won't touch anything," Mel said.

"Why don't I stay out here?" Lisa said.

"You'll be our lookout," Mel said as she followed Conner inside.

Once inside, Conner turned on the flashlight. They walked across the kitchen floor to the living room.

"This is where I was the other day," Mel said.

"Did you notice anything about the kitchen when we walked through it?" he asked.

"No," she said.

He turned around and went back into the kitchen. The floor creaked and the wood gave a little as he walked over it.

"That doesn't feel right," he said.

He ran the flashlight around the floor. There was an

area rug under his feet. He handed the flashlight to Mel, moved off the rug, and rolled it up. Someone had cut a piece of the vinyl flooring out, exposing a plywood floor underneath. The rectangular piece looked newer. It had an edge, indicating it was not part of the original floor.

"This part has been replaced," Conner said. "It looks pretty new, too."

"Why would he cut a hole in the kitchen floor?" Mel asked.

"Why would a dog try to dig around the edge of the home?"

"Oh, God," Mel said. "He couldn't have."

Conner rolled the rug back in place. "Let's go."

She wanted to look in her aunt's bedroom, but Conner was leaving. As he walked to the door, he brushed against the wall and Mel heard something fall to the floor. She picked it up. It was a key ring full of keys. She kept it and when she got outside, put it in her purse.

"What happened?" Lisa asked.

"That Jason guy cut a hole in the kitchen floor," Mel said.

"Why would he do that?" Lisa asked.

"To hide something," Mel said.

"But this thing," Lisa waved at the home, "doesn't sit on the ground."

"He'd have to stand in the hole and dig so no one would see him," Conner said.

"What was he trying to hide?" Lisa said. She sensed Mel was upset. "Oh."

Mel was quiet. She could feel tears forming in her eyes and didn't want to cry in front of Conner. She thought about Nana Grace. She didn't want to have to tell her Audrey was gone.

"Let's go," she said and began to walk away. Conner went after her.

"We're gonna find out what happened," he said as he grabbed her arm. "I won't let this go."

"Yeah, I know," she said, trying not to look at him.

"I'll call you tomorrow."

Mel nodded and pulled her arm away. Lisa passed Conner and waved.

"Nice meeting you," she said.

Conner put out his hand and touched her arm. "Keep an eye on her."

"I will," Lisa said.

"I mean it. Don't let her come back here alone. She's gonna get in trouble. We need to do this right so we can get this guy. She could screw up the investigation."

"And here I thought you cared about her."

"Just take care of her."

Lisa left him and caught up to Mel. "Hey," she said. "Are you okay?"

"No," Mel said. "I just want to go home."

"What do you say we stop at the drugstore, buy a pint of Ben and Jerry's, and go back to the condo and sit on the porch?"

Mel smiled. "That sounds good."

Chapter Seventeen

WHEN THEY GOT BACK TO THE CONDO, MEL AND LISA changed into their sleep shirts. They took their ice cream and went to the porch. Despite Mel's misgivings regarding the temperatures, it was warm, and there was a nice breeze coming off the Gulf of Mexico. Lisa lit the citronella candle on the small table between their lounge chairs.

"I couldn't see him very well, but in the dark, that guy looked hot."

"He's cute," Mel said. "He believes me."

"What?"

"He didn't brush me off when I filed the report. He's been looking into it. He obviously thinks Audrey is…"

"I'm glad you're here."

"Would you really have gone to a club alone?" Mel asked.

"No. But I would have told you I did."

"Why?" Mel asked.

"I wouldn't want you to think I was a wuss."

"I wouldn't think that."

Lisa swirled her spoon over the surface of the ice cream. "Are you still leaving tomorrow?"

"I'm not sure. I want to see what happens, but Sunday is Christmas."

"You could stay here. We could do Christmas together."

"I don't know. I'm always with my grandmother on Christmas."

"So call her and see what she says. We could go to the movies and eat popcorn."

"What about your dad?" Mel asked.

"Barcelona."

"Oh, that's right." Mel took a few bites. "What were you gonna do here alone?"

"Pretty much what I'd do with you. Go to a movie and eat popcorn."

Mel looked over at her friend. It was hard to tell what she was thinking in the low light from the candle. She sounded okay, but who's really okay with being alone at Christmas? Grandma would be with her mother, Nana Grace. Mel could always go home the day after Christmas.

"I'll stay here," Mel said. "I really want to find out what happened to Audrey. I'll just change my flight."

Lisa smiled. "It'll be nice having some company."

When Conner got home, he called his friend Mike, the K-9 officer.

"I want to ask a favor. Are you working tomorrow?"

"Yeah. Mark gave me Christmas Eve off this year."

"I need Rusty for about fifteen minutes tomorrow morning. Early, like seven."

"Should I wear my uniform?"

Conner thought for a minute. "No. It's not official."

"Which means Mark doesn't know about it."

"Yeah, and I have to do this before court begins."

"Shit."

"I'm working a missing person's case," Conner said.

"And you think the person is dead."

"I think she's buried under a mobile home."

"Great."

"If Rusty reacts, we'll take it to Mark."

"You'll take it to Mark. I'm gonna play dumb."

"I'll take it to Mark."

"Where is it?"

"Holiday Oaks. Number 298."

"I'll meet you there at seven."

THE NEXT DAY, CONNER'S SHIFT BEGAN AT NOON. HE brought his uniform with him so he could change at the sheriff's office. He arrived at Audrey's home at seven and saw Mike standing next to his own car, which was parked in front of Marge's home. He had a leash in his hand. Rusty was in the back seat. Rusty was a trained cadaver dog. He was a blonde German shepherd, a beautiful dog with an amazing nose. Mike also cared for another dog trained to detect drugs.

Conner parked behind Mark and went over to him.

"He's been antsy since we got here," Mike said.

"He might just smell the dog we found buried behind the home."

"Could be." Mike opened the door and put the leash on Rusty. "Come on, boy."

Rusty pulled Mike across the street.

"He smells something," Mike said.

The dog didn't fool around. He went straight up the driveway to the center of the home. He pulled hard on the leash when he reached the spot under the hole in the kitchen floor, then he started to bark.

"Shit," Conner said. "I was hoping he wouldn't find anything."

"You gotta tell Mark."

"I can't use this. I don't have probable cause."

"You do now."

"But we didn't get a warrant."

"What made you think there was somebody buried here in the first place?"

Conner hesitated. "The guy who lived here killed a dog."

"And?"

"I promised the girl who filed the missing persons I'd find out what happened to her aunt."

"And she's cute."

"That's not why. Well, maybe a little, but when I came by and talked to the guy, something didn't feel right. The more I found out about him, the less I liked him."

"You gotta go to Mark. I think you have probable cause."

"But I didn't have a damn warrant."

"So, I tell Mark I'm cutting through the park with Rusty on my way to Ulmerton Road and he goes crazy. I stop and let him do his thing. He smells decaying flesh under a mobile home. It just happens to be the one that guy lives in."

"You'd do that?" Conner said.

"We gotta see if there's a body here."

"Yeah, we do."

Mike took Rusty back to his car. He waved at Conner when he drove off. It was seven forty-five. Conner wanted to be in court when Jason was arraigned. He got in the car and drove to the sheriff's office.

MEL GOT UP AND GOT DRESSED. IT WAS NINE. LISA WAS still asleep. Mel wanted coffee but didn't feel like making it. She grabbed her purse and left the condo.

She headed to the mobile home park, stopping at a Starbucks drive-thru to get a tall coffee. When she got to the park, she sat in front of Marge's home until her coffee was gone, then she got out and went to Audrey's door.

She looked around before trying all the keys to see which one would open the door. The third try was the charm, and the door opened.

She looked at the floor when she stepped inside. The rug hid the cutout well. She went past it and turned right. She found Audrey's bedroom and looked around.

The bed was made. There was nothing on either end table. The room was meticulous.

She went to the dresser and started going through the drawers. Audrey's things were neatly folded and organized. She then went to the closet. Audrey's clothes were still there.

Mel looked around the room for a handbag. She saw one by the side of the bed. She sat on the bed and picked it up. She hated opening another woman's bag. It seemed like such a violation of Audrey's privacy, but she had to see if it had a wallet inside. She opened it.

Audrey's wallet was inside. Mel began to tear up again. Audrey wouldn't have gone somewhere without her wallet. Inside was her driver's license. The picture showed an elderly woman with a smile. Her hair was neatly done and she wore a touch of makeup. Tears began to roll down Mel's cheeks.

There were credit cards and a debit card from Regions Bank. She thought it was strange that Jason hadn't touched them. There were pictures of Grace and Laura, a library card, and some dollar bills inside, too.

She was putting the things back into the purse when she heard something. She got up and walked to the bedroom door. She listened. Someone was trying to get the kitchen door open.

She ran down the hall and across the living room to the sliding glass door. She stepped onto the porch and was about to go out the screen door when she saw Marge hobbling across the street.

"You bastard," she yelled. "You killed my Maurice."

Mel watched her pass the porch.

"Go away before I call the cops," Jason said.

"You killed my dog, you son of a bitch."

Mel heard something and then Jason yelled. "Ow. Get away from me."

He must have pushed her. "Don't you touch me," Marge said. Mel looked up and saw the man next door looking out his door. He'd seen her, too. She stuck her head out the porch's screen door and saw Marge hitting Jason with her cane. Thankfully, Jason's back was to her, so he didn't see Mel leaving the porch and coming up behind him. She walked past him, went to Marge, and grabbed her arms.

"Marge, stop," she said.

"He killed my dog!" Marge cried. Mel could smell alcohol on her.

"Marge, come home," Mel said.

Jason had grabbed the cane. He pulled it out of Marge's hand and she fell back. Mel caught her.

"Take this old bat and get out of here," Jason said.

"Give her back her cane."

"She'll just hit me again."

"She can't walk without it. How can she leave you alone if she can't walk?"

He threw the cane to the ground and went to his door. Mel couldn't remember if she had locked it or not. He put the key in and turned it. It opened and he went inside.

"Can you stand a minute while I get your cane?" Mel said.

"He killed my dog," Marge said.

"Right."

Mel bent over and picked it up while Marge swayed. Mel put the cane in Marge's hand. She kept her hand on Marge's arm as she walked her back across the street.

Chapter Eighteen

MEL GOT MARGE BACK TO HER HOME AND WENT INSIDE with her. There were dirty dishes in the sink and on the counter. She looked at Marge. Her hair was disheveled and her housedress stained.

"Where is Sharon?" Mel asked.

"She lives in St. Pete," Marge said. She was unsteady, so Mel guided her to the recliner in the living room. Marge sat and leaned her cane against the wall. It was an electrically powered chair and she pushed a button to raise her feet.

"Do you have her phone number?"

"Of course I have her phone number. What a thing to ask."

"Sorry. Where is it?"

Marge pointed a finger at her head and tapped. "I got it all up here."

Mel pulled out her phone. "Can you tell me what it is?"

Marge shook her head. "I don't want her here."

"But you shouldn't be alone after what happened."

"I don't want her here!" Marge cried. "Old busy-body. She hides my booze."

Marge reached for a pack of cigarettes lying on the end table by her chair. Mel lunged at her and grabbed them.

"Give me my smokes!" Marge protested.

"Maybe you should take a nap," Mel said.

"Maybe you should go to hell."

Mel kept the cigarettes as she walked to the kitchen. Marge yelled for her to come back. Mel looked for an address book, or card on the fridge – something that would have Sharon's number on it. She couldn't leave the old woman alone. Marge was drunk. If she went after Jason again, she could be arrested, or worse, hurt. He was pretty pissed off when she came after him.

Mel found a handwritten note on the fridge with Sharon's number on it. It looked new. She must have posted it there the other day when she was with Marge. Mel dialed the number.

"Hello," Sharon said.

"Hi. I met you the other day when you were at Marge's house. My name is Mel."

"I remember you."

"Marge went after Jason Frye this morning," Mel said. "She's had something to drink."

"Darn," Sharon said. "I guess I should come. I was hoping to get my Christmas shopping done. What's she doing now?"

Marge was grumbling about her cigarettes. "She's in her recliner."

"Does she look like she might go to sleep?"

Mel looked at Marge. She looked a little frisky to her.

"Not really," Mel said.

"Okay. I'll come over. Can you stay there for a few

minutes? It takes me about a half hour to get there, but if she falls asleep, you can leave her alone."

"Sure," Mel said, rolling her eyes.

"Thank you. I really appreciate it."

Mel hung up the phone and looked at Marge. She was crying.

"Hey, Marge," Mel said. "What's wrong?"

"He killed my dog," Marge said.

Mel walked over to a chair near the recliner and sat.

"Maurice was a good dog," Mel said. "How old was he?"

"He was ten. He was just a baby."

"What kind of dog was he?" Mel asked. She had seen dogs like Maurice but couldn't remember what they were called.

"He was a shih tzu," Marge said. "The sweetest dog ever."

"He was pretty."

"He was."

Mel thought about Audrey. "Do you know anything about that guy, Jason?"

"Son of a bitch," Marge said.

"Yes, he is, but do you know anything about him?"

"I know he killed my dog."

"Do you think he hurt Audrey?"

"Damn straight he did. Him and his no good father."

This is interesting, Mel thought. Why hadn't Marge mentioned the father before? "What did his father do?"

"He came around the pool."

"Really? When?"

"Who knows? I heard it from Dick."

"Who's Dick?" Mel asked.

"Dick. You know. The guy next to her house."

"On which side?"

"Next to the street."

Dick had to be the man living in number 300.

"He told you Jason's father came to the pool?"

"Yeah. He was talking up the ladies. He was looking for a mark if you ask me."

"And Audrey took the bait?"

Marge laughed. "Like a rat to a sewer."

Why would Audrey fall for Jason Sr.'s bullshit? Mel thought. "When did he start coming around her house?"

"Who knows? Months ago. She'd get all dolled up like a geisha."

Oh, brother, Mel thought. "Did he ever live in that home?"

"Nah. But I haven't seen the old one for a while. He used to come to her house and bring the kid. I guess they ate dinner there."

Mel tried to think of something to ask, then she thought of the hole in the kitchen floor.

"Did you ever hear anything weird coming from the house?"

"Like what?" Marge asked.

"Like a power saw."

Marge laid her head back and looked at the ceiling. "No. My ears aren't so good anymore. But Dick got real mad one day. He came over and sat on my porch."

"Why was he mad?"

"The kid was playing his music real loud. Dick was mad. He told the manager, but Bea never did a thing. She had cancer. No one was supposed to know, but Peggy told me when I dropped off my rent."

Mel remembered talking to Peggy the first day. "Is that why Bea left?"

"Yeah. She was pretty sick. Peggy was mad because she

wasn't doing her job. Stuff was piling up. She wasn't running credit checks on new residents, stuff like that."

So that's how Jason Sr. was able to sign a lease for Audrey's home, Mel thought. From the look of his mobile home, Mel didn't think he would have been able to pass a credit check. That's why Jason junior was able to move in without anyone asking about him.

"Did you know that Audrey sold the home to him?"

"What?" Marge said. She looked incredulous.

"She signed the title over to him."

"No way. Huh-huh. Audrey may have been a bitch, but she wasn't stupid."

Mel got mad. She didn't like Marge calling her aunt a bitch. She took a few deep breaths to keep from punching her. "I saw the title."

"No. I don't believe she'd do it. He was a swindler."

"Right. But he did, and Jason junior moved in."

"Yeah. I complained about that. Bea said he was Audrey's caretaker."

"Did Bea talk to Audrey?"

"Who knows?"

"Do you think Peggy would know?"

"She knows everything that happens here."

But she didn't know Jason was living in Audrey's home.

Mel saw something through the window behind Marge's chair. She hoped it was Sharon. She got up and went to the window. She saw Conner get out of his cruiser.

Chapter Nineteen

MEL FELT THE CIGARETTES IN HER POCKET. "I HAVE TO GO outside," she said. "You stay here."

"Don't you tell me what to do," Marge said.

"Fine," Mel said.

She went out the kitchen door and over to the cruiser. There was another officer with Conner. They had both gotten out of the cruiser and were standing near it.

"Hey," she said.

Conner turned and looked surprised to see her.

"What are you doing here?" he asked.

"It's a long story."

"I got a search warrant," he said smiling.

"How?" she asked.

"I'll catch you up later," he said. "Is that your car?" he pointed to her rental.

"Yeah," she said.

"Would you move it? We have more cars coming."

"Are you gonna arrest him?"

"Depends on what we find."

Mel had left her purse inside Marge's home and went

back to retrieve her keys. She moved the car to the main road running through the park, then went back to Marge's.

"You want to sit on the porch?" she asked Marge.

"Not without Maurice."

"The cops are going to search Audrey's home."

"Yeah? Let's sit on the porch."

Another cruiser arrived, then a K-9 cruiser car with a white dog in the back seat. Conner was knocking on the door of Audrey's home. She could see inside the porch and saw Jason opening the sliding glass door. He saw the police car and went back inside.

The deputy with the dog got out of his car. He took the dog out. The dog was pulling on his leash. He went straight to the driveway and barked when he reached the space under the kitchen. One of the deputies was taking notes.

Conner was banging on the door. Jason finally answered and Conner handed him the paper warrant. He must have asked Jason to step outside. He did, and one of the deputies stayed with him while three went inside.

"He's shitting in his pants," Marge said. "Dog killer. You're gonna get yours now."

Sharon appeared on the sidewalk coming toward Marge's home. She looked annoyed.

"I had to park way up the street," she said when she got to the porch. "What's going on?"

"He's getting his," Marge said.

"They're searching the house," Mel said.

"Is it drugs?" Sharon asked. "I always smelled marijuana when I came here. I'll bet that kid sells it."

"Pot head asshole," Marge said.

"Marge!" Sharon cried. "Language."

"What? Like she's never heard it before?"

"Thank you for staying," Sharon said.

"No problem. Do you mind if I stay for a little longer?"

"You want to see what happens?"

"If you don't mind," Mel said.

"How much longer?" Sharon asked.

"Go do your shopping," Mel replied.

Sharon left, promising to return within an hour. A half hour after she left, a car arrived and parked in front of number 300. Two people in uniform got out. The car had "Forensics" written on the side.

Mel had seen several episodes of CSI and knew why they were here. She felt sadness overwhelming her. Marge had fallen asleep. Mel tried to focus on seeing Audrey sitting in a lounge chair on the deck of a ship sipping one of those drinks with an umbrella in it, but the image vanished when Conner and another officer came outside carrying a large piece of wood.

Conner walked across the street and up to the porch.

"We found something. The forensic team is going to start digging. You should probably leave now."

"I promised Sharon I'd stay with Marge. I want to be here."

Conner nodded. "Mel, it doesn't look good."

She started crying again. Conner put his hand out and she took it.

"I'm sorry," he said.

"It's not over yet," Mel said.

"I gotta get back."

"Okay. I'm okay."

Her phone rang and she took it out of her pocket. It was Nana Grace. She couldn't talk to her now. She let it go to voicemail.

Mel watched the forensic team carry shovels into the house. She decided Conner was right – she didn't want to see what would happen next. She went inside Marge's home and turned on the TV. She was tired. She had been up late with Lisa and woke up too early. Despite her growing anxiety, she fell asleep.

Mel woke up when Sharon arrived.

"You okay?" she asked.

"I'm fine," Mel said.

"I'm here now if you want to go."

Mel nodded and got up. She grabbed her purse. She reached into her pocket and handed Sharon Marge's cigarettes.

"Thanks for staying with her," Sharon said. "Merry Christmas."

Mel had forgotten it was almost Christmas. "Merry Christmas." She'd also forgotten to cancel her flight home.

As she walked outside, she saw two people carrying something out of Audrey's home. It was a large, black bag. A body bag. Mel began to sob. The deputy with the dog came to her.

"Are you Mel?" he asked.

"Yes," she said between gulps of air.

"I'm sorry," he said. "We think we found someone."

She nodded.

"Conner just took the man living here to the sheriff's office. He asked me to stay and tell you."

"Thanks," she said.

"We won't know for sure until they do an autopsy. Are you gonna be all right to drive?"

She nodded, but she wasn't sure herself.

"I can take you."

"No. I'll be all right. We don't even know for sure it's her."

"Please don't drive until you calm down. I really shouldn't let you."

"I'm fine. I'm going to stay a few more minutes."

He put his hand on her shoulder, then went back to his cruiser. He waited until Mel went to her car and got inside before driving away. She cried for a few minutes before pulling herself together and starting the car.

As she drove to the park entrance, her phone rang. She parked on the side of the road and looked at it. It was Lisa.

"Hey," she said when she answered.

"Hi," Lisa said. "Where are you?"

"I'm at my aunt's park."

"Oh. Are you coming back here? You sound kind of down."

Mel started crying again. "I think they found my aunt."

"Oh, Mel. It's gonna be all right."

"I know. I don't want to talk about it."

"Just come back. Be careful driving."

"I'm fine."

Chapter Twenty

An unrepentant Jason Frye sat in the interrogation room. His hands were cuffed. Conner was watching him from behind the mirrored panel that separated them. Jason hadn't said a word while being taken to the sheriff's office, even after he was informed they had found a body buried under his mobile home.

A detective, Jerry Klein, arrived and went into the interrogation room. Jason looked up, but he didn't look scared. He was smiling. Conner felt like punching him in the face.

"So, we found a body buried under your trailer," Jerry said. Jason didn't reply. "And we think we know who it is. Why did you kill her, Jason?"

"I didn't kill her," Jason said.

"Then why bury her under the house?"

"I didn't kill her," Jason repeated. He looked at Jerry's pocket. "Can I have a smoke?"

"Later. Right now I want to know why you buried her under the trailer."

Jason put his hands on the table. "I liked her. She was nice to me."

"You must have liked her a lot to keep her with you so long. The coroner said she must have been under there for months."

"She was old, you know?"

Jerry sat back in his chair. He looked at Jason. His rap sheet included a possession and some traffic tickets. Jerry was trying to figure out what would make this guy kill someone.

"But it's hard living with an old person, isn't it, Jason? They are so needy."

"Audrey was nice to me. She was no trouble at all. She liked me."

"Then why did you kill her?"

"Is that what the coroner said?" Jason cried. "Did he say I killed her?"

"We won't know until he's done with the autopsy. Did she piss you off? Did you hit her hard enough to knock her down? Maybe she hit her head and you didn't know what to do."

"I want a lawyer," Jason said. "And I didn't kill her."

Jerry kept hammering Jason, but the kid had clammed up. He didn't say another word.

When Jerry emerged from the interrogation room, Conner stopped him.

"Was she hit on the head?" he asked.

"I don't know. I was just fishing. The medical examiner is backed up. It may have to wait until after Christmas."

"What did forensics say?" Conner asked.

"Not much. Jeannie said she didn't see any cracks in the skull, but the victim was old. She could have bled out from a wound without cracking her skull."

"Why do you think he did it?" Conner asked.

"Between us, I think she died and he panicked. He had a nice setup there. A roof over his head and her Social Security coming in every month."

"Did they find blood anywhere?"

"Jeannie said no."

Conner frowned. "I have to talk to her niece. Is there any way to get the autopsy pushed up?"

"Not with Christmas. The doc won't work on the holiday."

"He has assistants, doesn't he?"

"Conner, this isn't the crime of the century. Let it go. He'll get it done."

Jerry walked away, leaving Conner alone in front of the window. Jason was tapping his fingers on the table. He didn't look worried, and that worried Conner. Either the kid was a sociopath, or he didn't kill Audrey.

He could be charged with unlawful burial and fraud regarding the Social Security, and that might put him away for a while, but it didn't seem right. When Audrey's family found out, it would be devastating. He deserved to go away for a long time.

A deputy came and took Jason out of the interrogation room. He'd take Jason to a cell. He'd be transferred to the Pinellas County Jail and put in general population. When the state attorney decided what he'd be charged with, he'd be arraigned, assigned bail, and given a public defender.

Conner wondered how he had gotten out of jail that morning. He'd been arraigned on the animal cruelty charge and someone must have bonded him out. He went to his desk and looked at the court docket. Jason was bonded out by a bail bondsman on 49th Street, a block away from the jail. He dialed their number and found out that Susan, Jason's girlfriend at the water company, had paid the ten percent on Jason's thousand dollar bond.

"And I thought you didn't see him anymore," Conner said out loud when he hung up the phone.

"Did you catch that body under the trailer case?" Jim, the deputy at the next desk, asked.

"Yes. I was following up on the missing persons I got the other day."

"That was dumb luck, wasn't it? I guess you found 'em."

Sadly, Conner hoped so too, although he would have preferred finding out she was in Europe.

Chapter Twenty-One

LISA WAS CHATTERING, BUT MEL WASN'T LISTENING. THEY were sitting on the porch. The sky was overcast and it looked like it would rain soon.

"So, what do you want to do for Christmas?" Lisa asked.

"I'm sorry," Mel said. "I wasn't listening."

Lisa smiled. "That's okay. I just don't know what to say to you."

"You don't have to say anything. Just be here."

"How well did you know your aunt?"

"That's just it. I didn't know her well at all, but I've been close to my grandmother and I know this will hurt her terribly. I don't want to have to tell her, but I'm gonna have to."

"It might be better if you just do it and get it over with. She should know."

"But I'd rather tell her after Christmas, you know? Won't it ruin Christmas for her for the rest of her life?"

"Yeah, I guess it would. Your aunt didn't just go to sleep. She was buried under that place."

Mel glared at Lisa. "I know."

"Sorry. I'm not real good with things like this. Would you like me to leave you alone for a while? I could run to the store and get stuff for later."

"I wish Conner would call," Mel said.

"It's Christmas Eve. Is he working?"

"I thought he would call last night. I left a message on his voicemail. I don't want to call again or he'll think I'm stalking him."

"One call doesn't make you a stalker. Call him again."

"Maybe he doesn't want to tell me what happened. Maybe it's so awful he can't say the words."

"He's a cop. He has to be busy."

"But he's called me all along. Why stop now?"

"Mel, call him. I'm going to the store. Do you want anything?"

"Bring ice cream," Mel said. "I need chocolate."

After Lisa left, Mel grabbed her phone from the table between the loungers. She noticed the call from Nana Grace and felt bad she hadn't called her back. Lisa had given her a Benadryl when they came back to the condo and Mel had slept for hours. She would call Nana Grace after she talked to Conner. She dialed his number. This time he picked it up.

"Hi," Mel said.

"Sorry I haven't called. I've been trying to get someone to do the autopsy and I'm hitting walls."

"They haven't done it yet?"

"No. I'm afraid it won't be until after Christmas. I'm sorry, Mel. I really tried to get someone on it."

"So I can't call my grandmother yet because we don't even know for sure it is my aunt."

"Nothing positive yet. But by the end of next week, we will know."

"That means I have to stay here another week."

"You don't have to stay. I can call you."

"But I can't just leave her here."

"Oh. Well, no. Listen, I'm off tonight. Do you want to do something?"

"Lisa and I are staying in."

"Can I come over? My family lives in the Midwest."

"You can come, but I don't know if I'll be good company."

"Give me the address."

Mel gave him the address and hung up the phone. She looked at the water and sighed. She still didn't know if she should call Nana Grace. What if it wasn't Audrey's body? She would upset the old woman for no reason. She decided to wait. She'd have to call tomorrow to say Merry Christmas, but she'd have to say she still didn't know anything. She hoped Nana wouldn't press her for more information.

———

Lisa returned carrying a small, decorated Christmas tree that she set on the kitchen table.

"I saw it and couldn't resist," she said. "It lights up."

She plugged it into the outlet next to the table and smiled when the different colored lights came on.

"See," she said, "it's Christmas!"

Mel smiled. She was glad Lisa had brought it home. It did make it feel like Christmas.

"I have to call my grandmother tomorrow," Mel said. "I'm not sure I can keep this from her."

"You'll do fine. You're stronger than you think."

"I am when it comes to myself, but when it comes to her, I don't know. I don't know if I can stand to hear her cry."

"She's probably stronger than you think, too. Didn't you say she got a divorce? That was like a hundred years ago. It was hard to get one back then. She'd have to be strong to do that."

"It was sixty years ago. I guess she would have to be strong to do that then. I'm just chicken, I guess."

"Well, you don't have to do it until tomorrow so let's talk about something else."

Lisa emptied the bag of groceries and showed Mel the two half gallons of ice cream she had bought.

"The store had a buy one get one free sale. I got you rocky road and for me, vanilla fudge."

Mel took the half gallon of rocky road from Lisa's hand and took a spoon out of the drawer.

"I'll get you a bowl," Lisa said.

"I won't need one," Mel said. She took the half gallon to the living room.

"Okay, then."

Mel was able to eat half the carton before she surrendered to her full stomach and put the rest in the freezer.

"I feel sick," she said.

"You want to walk around the block?" Lisa said.

"Why would I want to do that? I said I feel sick."

"It would move it through your stomach."

"I don't think that will work. It feels like a brick in my stomach."

"I got nothing else. So, do you want to go to a movie tomorrow?"

"We could. I just have to see what happens when I talk to my nana."

"How old is she?"

"I'm not sure exactly, but I know she's in her nineties. My mother is in her forties, and my grandmother is in her sixties."

"What happened with your mother? I remember she used to visit you once in a while."

"I don't see her," Mel said. She thought about her mother. "Did I ever tell you about her? She got pregnant when she was in high school and when I was born, my grandmother raised me while she finished school. I don't think she had any interest in being a mom. She would come home on holidays and talk to me like I was one of her friends. It pissed me off. She treated my grandmother like shit."

"I remember the one time I saw her, she was trying to dress like you. Why didn't your grandmother tell her off?"

"Because grandma didn't want her to mess with the custody arrangement. My mother still had parental rights. Grandma didn't want her to pull something stupid like taking me away from her."

"But if she didn't want you, what difference would it have made?"

"There was something between them I never understood, and neither one of them would talk about it."

"That sucks. But I'm glad you stayed with your grandma because I wouldn't have met you if you'd been with your mother."

"I would have liked living in California, though. I don't like the cold. But, yeah, I'm glad I met you, too."

"When is Conner coming over?"

"I guess after work. He didn't say exactly."

"I bought a frozen lasagna and two bottles of soda."

"That sounds nutritious."

"Says the woman who ate a half gallon of rocky road. We're on vacation, Mel."

"I know. I don't know if I can eat another thing today."

"Then Conner and I will eat it, while we gaze into each other's eyes."

Mel laughed. "He does have nice eyes." She put her hands on her stomach. She could feel her full stomach and noted how hard it was. "Do we have anything for indigestion?"

"I think my dad has some Pepto Bismol in one of the medicine cabinets."

"Oh, God, no. Not that pink stuff."

"I can go get something. There's a Walgreen's down the street."

"No. I'll be all right."

"Come on," Lisa said. "We'll go for a walk."

She went to Mel and pulled her out of the chair. Mel groaned, but followed Lisa. They went down the stairs to the street and went to the beach. The overcast sky cloaked the full sun, giving the illusion of UV ray safety. Lisa had put on her sunblock when she got dressed, but Mel hadn't thought of it, and when they returned to the condo, she was a nice, bright red.

"I'm going to the drugstore," Lisa said.

"Why?" Mel asked.

"Because you'll need some aloe vera, and I'll pick up some antacid, too."

Mel went to the bathroom mirror and looked at her face. She came back to the living room.

"Okay," she said, "and thanks."

"I should have reminded you to cover your skin. I'll be back."

Now Mel was not only depressed, she was sore and sick to her stomach. She thought about calling Conner and telling him not to come, but he had no family here. He'd be alone. She looked at her phone and saw that it was four. She might feel better in three hours.

Chapter Twenty-Two

MEL DID FEEL BETTER WHEN CONNER ARRIVED AT SEVEN-thirty. She didn't eat much lasagna, though, and sipped coke for her stomach. Conner and Lisa ate well, and when they were done, Conner put one of the kitchen chairs on the porch so they could all sit together. Lisa lit the citronella candle.

"Why can't they do an autopsy sooner?" Lisa asked.

"Because the M.E. has the holiday off. He's a doctor."

"So, of course, he has off," Lisa said.

"Of course," Conner said. "You really got red."

Mel smiled, but it hurt her cheeks. "I did. Thanks for reminding me."

Conner smiled broadly. "Don't mention it. This is Florida, you know."

"Be nice," Lisa said. "She's in pain."

"And it's Christmas," Mel said.

"Okay. But it is Florida."

"You said your family is in the Midwest. Where-abouts?" Mel asked.

"Missouri. It gets cold there."

"Like Jersey," Mel said. "I hate the cold."

"I thought I'd be near Miami," Conner said. "I should have looked at a map."

"How did you get the job here?" Lisa asked.

"My friend lived here. He told me they were taking applications and I applied."

"Were you a cop in Missouri?" Lisa asked.

"For a while. I went into the academy after I got my associate's degree."

"Do you like it?" Mel asked.

"It's never dull," Conner said.

"Do you think it's her?"

Conner looked at Mel. "Yes."

"I have to tell my grandmother something. I just want to be right when I talk to her."

"I told her to just say Merry Christmas," Lisa said.

"I know she'll ask me outright if I know anything. I'm a terrible liar."

"Don't lie. Just say the police are working on it and you haven't heard anything," Conner said. "Period. Don't elaborate or she'll trip you up."

"Yeah," Lisa said. "The less you say, the better."

"We'll know by next week, Mel."

"How?" Mel asked.

"DNA. You're a relative. We'll swab you and match it to hers."

"Oh."

"So, are we going to a movie tomorrow or what?" Lisa asked.

"I have to work," Conner said.

"I don't know if I'll want to or not," Mel said.

"Well, this sucks," Lisa said. "I think I'll go to bed."

Conner looked at his watch. "It's only nine o'clock."

"I'm tired. I'll see you. Nice meeting you, Conner."

"You, too."

After Lisa left, Conner sat on her lounger. He looked over at Mel's red face. She looked like a sad little girl.

"When are you due back at work?" he asked.

"After new year's."

"You said you manage the place. What's that like?"

"It's hard because people don't listen. They don't show up on time. They want to wear me down so I'll let them have their way."

"So you're like a parent."

"Oh, God. Absolutely."

"There are Starbucks down here," Conner said.

She glanced at him. "So."

"So you could transfer and be warm."

"I can't really leave my grandmother. Both of them actually."

"Bring them with you."

"Nana just moved into a senior complex. I doubt they want to move again. And Nana is very attached to Jersey."

"So you'll stay in Jersey."

"Yeah, Jersey."

Mel's phone rang. She grabbed it off the table and looked at it.

"It's my grandmother," she said. She touched the phone. "Hello."

"Hi, Mel," her mother said. "It's mom. I wanted to wish you a Merry Christmas."

"I thought you were in California."

"I was. I came to visit for Christmas. I'm disappointed you're not here."

"Oh. Well, Merry Christmas."

"So you're in Florida."

"Yeah. I'm with Lisa."

"Who is that, your friend?"

"Only since my freshman year in high school."

"You don't have to get snippy."

"Then maybe we should cut this short."

"God, Mel. Can't you ever be civil with me?"

"Have a happy new year, Mom. I have company. See ya."

Mel hung up the phone before her mother could reply. She felt so angry. Her grandmother hadn't told Mel her mother was coming to New Jersey. She probably thought Mel would be home by now and knew Mel wouldn't come to her apartment if she knew her mother was there. What a screwed-up family she had.

"That was your mom?" Conner asked.

"Yeah. She's at my grandmother's place."

"What does she do?"

"She's a hairdresser on some TV show. She lives in California."

"So you don't see her very much."

"Never, in fact. And she doesn't understand why I have so little respect for her."

"She is your mom."

"Tell her that."

Mel felt like finishing the half gallon of rocky road, but her stomach lurched at the thought. Why did people always remind her that a parent deserved respect? Didn't they have to earn it like everyone else?

"I'm sorry. My mom was never home because she wasn't interested in me. She left me with my grandmother and never looked back. She sent money, and would show up a couple of times a year, but she was never my mother. So don't defend her to me, okay?"

"Okay. I didn't mean anything."

A feeling of guilt washed over her. She sighed.

"I know. Let's just forget about her."

"Tell me about your grandmother."

"She was the one who raised me. She was good at it, too."

"Who is Audrey's sister?"

"My Nana. She lived a few blocks away from where I grew up. I used to see her all the time. She was fun. She'd say outrageous things to shock us."

"I didn't have grandparents. My parents were in their forties when I was born. They were in their sixties when I graduated. I'm not sure they liked me leaving Missouri."

"They get a little clingy when you're the only kid."

"Exactly."

The sky had cleared and the stars were shining. They didn't talk for a while. They listened to the waves lapping the shore. It was peaceful, and before she knew it, Mel had fallen asleep.

Conner looked over and saw her face in the soft candlelit glow. He sat there a few minutes, then got up, picked her up, and carried her inside to her bed.

"Merry Christmas, Mel," he said. He kissed her on the forehead and pulled the blanket over her.

He blew out the candle, closed the sliding glass door, and made sure the oven was turned off before he left by the kitchen door. He turned the knob before he went down the stairs to make sure it was locked. Then he went to his car and drove home.

Chapter Twenty-Three

MEL WOKE UP IN HER BED THE NEXT MORNING. HER ARMS and legs were stiff from sunburn, and she winced when she turned over. She got out of bed and went to find the aloe vera.

Lisa was sitting at the kitchen table.

"Merry Christmas," she said.

"Where did you put the aloe?" Mel asked.

"It's over here on the counter."

Mel went to the counter and found the big bottle of aloe vera gel. She squirted a generous portion onto her arms and then sat and put it on her legs. Lastly, she covered her face.

"You look sore," Lisa said.

"It hurts more today."

"Keep putting on the aloe."

"You wanted to go to the movies."

"It doesn't matter. I don't want to leave you alone."

"I'm sorry," Mel said.

"You didn't do it on purpose. You've had a hard week."

"Did you buy anything to eat for today?"

"No. But a lot of places are open here. Everyone is on vacation. This is when they make their money."

"I guess we can order in."

"We can sit on the porch, before the sun comes around and sets."

"Did it rain?" Mel asked.

"No. The clouds just went away."

Mel got up and hobbled to her phone, which was charging on the coffee table. She looked at it and saw that her grandmother Laura had called. She touched the phone and returned her call.

"Merry Christmas, Grandma," she said when Laura picked up.

"Merry Christmas. Did you listen to my message?"

"No. I just called you back."

"I'm afraid I have some bad news. Nana Grace passed away late last night."

"Oh, no," Mel said. Tears sprung in her eyes. She had never called her back.

"She went in her sleep. It was very peaceful."

"But she'll never know about Audrey."

"Do you know anything yet, dear?"

Shit, Mel thought. She hadn't planned on saying anything until she knew, but with Nana gone, she might as well tell her grandmother what she knew.

"The police searched her house and found something."

"What did they find?"

Mel took in a deep breath. "They found a body under the house. It was buried in the ground."

"Oh, dear," Laura said. "Do they know it's her?"

"The police aren't sure if it's Audrey or not. They won't know for another week."

"But they assume it is her."

"Yeah, I think so. They arrested the guy, the one who was living there."

"They did? That's good. I mean, who else could it be? If she's been murdered, that is."

"I feel so bad. I wanted Nana to know."

"It's better she didn't know. It would have hurt her to think of her sister that way."

"That's true. Oh, Grandma. I'm so sorry."

"I have to make the arrangements for Nana. Are you coming home?"

"I missed my flight and didn't cancel and rebook, so I'm not sure they'll let me use that ticket. I still have some money left from Nana to buy another one."

"I'm calling the funeral director tomorrow. I'll let you know the details when I do. Otherwise, how are you doing? Linda told me she called you."

"Yeah. What's up with that? You didn't tell me she was coming for Christmas."

"I was trying to spare you, dear."

"The conversation was tense."

"I'm sorry. I wanted you to come home and I knew if you knew she was here, you wouldn't."

"You always do this. You've got to let me decide for myself if I want to see her or not. You can't make a happy reunion because you want to."

"I know, but she's my daughter. And she does love you."

"I know. Is she still there? Or did she bug out when she heard Nana had died?"

"She's here. She's going to help me with the arrangements."

"Well, that's a first."

"Okay, Mel. I get it. You're upset. So, what are you doing today? I hope you're not alone."

"I'm with Lisa. She wants to go to a movie."

"Oh, that will be nice. Be careful driving."

"I will. What are you doing?"

"I'm staying home with Linda."

"I'm sorry about Nana, Grandma. Let me know about the funeral. Merry Christmas."

"I will and Merry Christmas to you."

Mel hung up. Lisa was pouring coffee from the coffeemaker.

"Why did you tell her we were going to the movies?"

"Because if she hears I'm all burned she'll worry."

"Didn't you just yell at her for hiding the truth about your mother?"

"This is different."

"How is this different?"

"It just is."

Lisa sat at the table and Mel poured herself a mug of coffee. She sat and was grateful the back of her thighs weren't burned.

"How did I get so red so fast?" she asked.

"It's those nasty rays, the ones that come through the clouds. We were out there for two hours."

"It was that long?"

"Yeah. We went all the way up to that resort and back."

"I'll never go outside without sunblock again."

"I should have said something. I never thought you wouldn't put it on. This is Florida."

"So I've been told."

Chapter Twenty-Four

By Tuesday, Mel's skin felt better. She didn't have to avoid bumping into things, and she felt like going out. Lisa drove and they went to lunch and movie. Sometime during the show, her grandmother called and left a message. The funeral would be held on Thursday. Mel went online and booked a flight out on Wednesday morning.

As she and Lisa walked out of the theater, Mel looked at her phone.

"I have to call Conner," Mel said.

"Yeah. What happened to him after I left you two on the porch?"

"I fell asleep and he put me to bed. I'm surprised he didn't call."

"Especially after that hot date."

"The only hot thing about it was my burn."

"So, call him."

"I hate to have to tell him I'm leaving."

"Why?" Lisa asked. She looked at Mel. "You like him."

"He's a nice guy."

"But he lives a thousand miles from you."

"So what? He's still a nice guy."

"But you can't have a relationship with him."

"Why not? People have long-distance relationships."

"People who've known each other a long time. Not people who just met a few days ago."

"I know. But I can dream, can't I?"

Mel's phone rang. It was Conner.

"Hi," she said.

"I got the M.E. to do the autopsy," he said.

She bit her lower lip. "What did he find out?"

"Can you come down here so we can swab your cheek?"

"That's right. You want DNA. Yeah, I can come. I'll be there in a few."

When she hung up, she told Lisa they had to go to the sheriff's office. She went online and booked a flight for Wednesday morning. The traffic was lighter, but there were still plenty of tourists in Clearwater Beach. Mel was happy to let Lisa drive.

When they parked, Mel saw Conner's car and felt her heart jump. She had tried to keep from feeling something for him, but it hadn't worked. She liked him. She was just glad he wouldn't be able to see her blush when she saw him.

She went to the window in reception and the woman behind the glass said that Conner was waiting for her. Conner came to the side door and she felt a tingle in her stomach. She followed him to his desk.

"All you have to do it rub this on the inside of your cheek," he said, handing her a long swab on a stick. She ran it over the inside of her cheek and handed it back to him. He placed it in a plastic tube with a stopper.

"We'll have them test this against the DNA from the body and we'll be able to identify her."

"It's a woman?" Mel asked.

"Yes. It was a woman. She'd been in there about three months. The M.E. said she died of natural causes."

"Then why try to hide her like that?"

"He wanted to stay in the home. He wanted her Social Security."

"Did he finally confess?"

"No, but it's the most likely reason. He's been drawing money from her bank account. He had his own debit card. He just took advantage of the situation."

"Poor Audrey. Oh…my Nana died, too. On Christmas Eve."

"I'm really sorry."

"I hadn't told her yet. I was going to after Christmas."

"Then I guess you have to go home."

She nodded. "I leave tomorrow morning."

"I'm off tomorrow. Can I take you to the airport?"

He looked hopeful. She shook her head. "I have a rental I have to return."

"I can follow you."

"Why would you want to do that?" she asked, hoping he would say he couldn't live without the sight of her face.

"So you won't be alone."

"That would be nice. I have to find out the time."

"Call me later."

She left him and turned to wave before going through the door. He was watching her. She went out in the parking lot and got into the car.

"Well," Lisa said.

"He wants to take me to the airport."

"See!" Lisa cried. "I knew he liked you."

"You never said that."

"Well, I did."

"It doesn't matter if he does or not. Like you said, we live a thousand miles apart."

"I know I said that, but you manage a Starbucks. You can live anywhere you want."

"I can't leave Grandma."

"Bring her with you. Don't old people love Florida?"

"She has a job, Lisa. She has her friends. Can we just go, please?"

Lisa started the car and pulled out of the spot. As they passed the entrance to the sheriff's office, Mel saw Conner. He had waited so he could wave to her again.

Chapter Twenty-Five

MEL'S BAG WAS PACKED AND SITTING BY THE FRONT DOOR of the condo. All Mel had to do was say goodbye to Lisa, who was in the shower.

Mel went out onto the porch and looked at the water. The beach was full of tourists, and kids were laughing and running into the small waves of the Gulf. She leaned on the porch rail and let the wind blow her hair. For one minute, she forgot why she had come to Florida and why she had to go home. She felt alive.

She breathed in the salt air and went back into the condo. Lisa was towel-drying her hair.

"I gotta go," Mel said.

Lisa wrapped the towel around her head and came to Mel. She put her arms around her and squeezed.

"Ow," Mel said. Lisa loosened her grip.

"I'm gonna miss you," she said.

"Me, too," Mel said. She squeezed Lisa back.

When they parted, Lisa looked into Mel's eyes. "Do you want me to come to the funeral? I can catch a flight tomorrow."

"You don't have to do that. You still have a few days here."

"A few days alone. That'll be fun."

"You don't have to come, but I'm not gonna tell you what to do."

"I'll see how I feel tonight when I'm sitting here with a pizza and a sad movie."

"Oh, stop," Mel said. "I have to go."

She went to the door and picked up her purse. Lisa came up behind her and picked up her bag.

"I can carry that," Mel said.

"Oh, just shut up and move," Lisa said.

Mel went out the door and down the steps with Lisa close behind.

"You don't have any shoes on," Mel said.

"Keep walking. This thing is heavy."

When they got near the car, Mel pushed the button on the key and opened the trunk. Lisa slipped the bag inside and closed it while Mel got into the driver's seat. Lisa came to the window and Mel rolled it down.

"Call me when you get there," Lisa said.

"I will. It's been fun."

"Oh yeah, especially the part where we broke into your aunt's house."

Mel smiled, then looked sad. "You're a good friend."

Lisa blushed. "I know, I know, now don't you have to get to the airport?"

"Conner said he would come."

Lisa looked around. "I don't see his car."

"I'm gonna wait for a minute."

"Um, this is awkward. My feet hurt. I'm gonna go back inside."

Lisa bent over and gave Mel another hug. "Have a safe trip."

Mel patted her arm. "Thanks for everything."

Lisa backed away, smiled, then went back to the condo. Mel sat a few minutes, watching the time go by on her phone. She really couldn't wait any longer. She didn't feel right about calling Conner. What if he had changed his mind? She decided to let him go and head to Tampa.

She dropped the car off in the rental return parking lot and headed for the terminal. After she checked her bag, she took the elevator to the second floor where the gates were located. She could get a cup of coffee at the Starbucks before heading to her gate.

She was in line waiting for her caramel macchiato when she felt a tap on her shoulder. She turned and saw Conner standing behind her.

"You made it!" she cried.

"I'm sorry. I got stuck doing paperwork last night and overslept."

"I've got two hours before I have to board."

"You just have to go through the line. I think I'll try flashing my badge so I can follow you out there."

She smiled. "Thanks for coming."

"I wanted to see you off. You've had a hard time."

The guy behind the counter took her order and Conner got a cup of coffee. They took their drinks to the seats by the elevators and sat.

"I've never been to New Jersey," he said.

"If you ever do, come in June. It's too cold and weird before that. July and August are nice, too."

"Three months of nice. What makes people stay there?"

"Philly and New York."

Conner laughed. "There has to be more to it than that."

"It has a great beach. Even in winter, I like the beach.

It's not the state so much as its location. I hate the cold. If it was warm there, I'd like it just fine."

"I've got some leave time saved up. I could visit and see that beach."

"Sure. And you could meet…"

She caught herself before she said "Nana." Her eyes welled with tears.

"I'm sorry," she said, brushing them aside. "I'm just, it's just too much, you know? They're both gone. I just talked to her. She sounded fine."

He reached out and took her hand. He couldn't think of anything to say.

She finished her coffee and checked the time. "I've gotta get to my gate."

They got up and Conner followed her to the gate. He flashed his badge, but the TSA worker frowned.

"Sorry, officer. Passengers only."

Conner took Mel's hand and pulled her to the side.

"I've got your number," he said. "Do you have mine?"

"In my phone."

"Call me when you get there. Don't feel stupid or something. Just call me. I want to hear your voice."

He bent down and kissed her. She blushed under her sunburn.

"I promise," she said when they parted.

"I'll come up in June."

"I'll take some time off."

"I like you. I know we haven't known each other long, but…"

"Oh, shut up," she said and kissed him again. She leaned back and smiled. "I have to go."

He walked with her back to the TSA worker and watched her walk down the hall to the shuttles. She turned once and waved. He waved back.

Chapter Twenty-Six

LAURA WAS TALKING TO AN OLDER WOMAN MEL HAD NEVER seen before. Most of the people at Grace's funeral were strangers to Mel, so she chose to sit near the wall and watch Laura make the rounds. Lisa had flown up in the middle of the night and was sitting next to her, but she was tired. She kept dozing off, and Mel would elbow her.

"What?" Lisa said.

"You were snoring."

"I don't snore."

"Well, you were breathing loudly."

There were more people at the funeral home than Mel had expected. Grace had been well-liked. Mel thought about Audrey and felt sad. She was not so well-liked, and Mel wondered what would happen when the coroner released her body for burial. She told Laura she would go to Florida and retrieve it, but Laura told her they would have Audrey cremated and shipped to New Jersey.

"You're not gonna have a funeral?" Mel said.

"We could have a memorial, but no funeral."

"Why not?"

"Because all her friends are in Florida. And I can't afford another funeral."

Mel felt sad for Audrey. She hoped when she was old, her grandchildren would have a funeral for her.

There was some commotion at the entrance to the room they were in and Mel strained her head to see what it was. Then she saw her, the only person who could completely ruin her day.

"Isn't that your mom?" Lisa said.

"Yeah."

Linda had overslept. She was dressed in jeans and a T-shirt. She also wore a multi-colored overcoat. She smiled at the mourners as she passed by, made a show of stopping in front of the casket, and then saw Mel. She put on her sad face and walked over to her daughter.

"Hi, Mel," she said, putting out her hands. Mel glared at her. She put down her hands and sat in the chair next to Mel.

"Hi, Mrs. Jones," Lisa said.

"Hello," Linda said, though it was clear she had no idea who Lisa was. "It's Ms." She looked at Mel. "I'm so glad I got to see you."

"Where else would I be?" Mel said. "Nana died. I'm here because I cared about her."

"I cared about her, too."

"Bullshit you did."

"How dare you talk to me that way!"

Mel shook her head and got up. She went to the ladies room with Linda following. Mel stood in front of the row of sinks and put her hands on the counter. She was still shaking her head when Linda walked in.

"I'm still your mother."

"Oh, can the act, Linda."

"What is wrong with you?"

"You, that's what's wrong with me. You show up here and expect me to be all 'Oh, mom, you came,' and I'm supposed to be all happy to see you. Well, I'm not."

"I didn't expect you to get on your knees and genuflect, but I did think you would be civil."

"Why? When was the last time I saw you, huh? Was it at my graduation? No, you had to work. Was it at my twentieth birthday party? No, you had to be on location in some third-world country."

"It's my job, Mel. If I don't go, I'll lose it, and they're hard to come by."

"It wouldn't have made any difference, Linda. You just don't give a shit about me and never have."

Linda smacked Mel across the face. Mel smacked her back.

"So, are we even now?" Mel asked. "Will you stay away from me?"

Mel was surprised to see the look in Linda's eyes. She looked hurt. She had to admit it felt good to hurt her. But when Linda started to cry, she did feel bad.

"Look, why don't we just not play this game anymore," Mel said.

"I'm your mother. I haven't been a good one, I'll admit that, but I do love you."

"You love your job, Linda. You have always put it first. Yeah, I get it, you can't afford to lose it, but you can afford to lose me."

"You'll understand things better when you're older."

"And I'll do the right thing and come to your funeral."

Mel walked past her and went back to her seat next to Lisa. She saw Linda go up to Laura and give her a hug. Laura looked annoyed. She had expected Linda to come earlier. Then she looked happy. If Linda could make her grandmother happy, then maybe Mel would give her a pass to future events. She'd try to make nice the next time they saw each other, for Laura's sake.

"What happened in there?" Lisa asked.

"I gave it to her."

"No wonder she looks so miserable."

"She's just surprised I noticed how neglectful she's been and called her on it."

"Be careful how you treat her. You may need a kidney one day, and she may be the only match."

Mel smiled. "Don't burn that bridge, huh?"

"Right. I mean it. No matter what, she's family. You don't have to see her, just make nice when you do."

"Why? So I can get her kidney one day? Do you know how hard it is for me to even look at her?"

"No. I've never been that pissed off at anybody."

"I'm not pissed off. I'm just tired of her thinking she can blow us off and then show up like nothing's wrong. She really hurts my grandmother, then she leaves and forgets all about us."

"Didn't she pay for your school?"

Mel sighed. "Yes."

"Well, that was something, wasn't it? Maybe she shows you she loves you that way."

"I don't doubt she loves me, Lisa. I just doubt she cares about me. I'm like this responsibility she can't shrug off. And she was legally bound to provide my education."

"What do you mean legally?"

"I mean Grandma got a court order saying she would have to pay for my education. Do you really think Linda would have otherwise?"

"I didn't know that."

"I know. It's embarrassing."

"I wonder why she showed up here?" Lisa asked.

"Who knows? I hope she leaves soon."

"Do you hate her?"

Mel watched Linda as she talked to another mourner. "No. I just don't like her is all."

"Do you love her?"

"I don't know. I know I'm supposed to love her, but she's so unlovable. She's missed every birthday, my graduation, every important event in my life. I doubt her friends in California even know she has a daughter. Why should I love her? Just because she gave birth to me?"

Lisa put her hand on Mel's and held it. "I'm sorry."

"Thanks for that. I gotta stop complaining. Grandma was a wonderful mother. I guess I'm just, oh shit, I am pissed off."

Mel chose to follow the limousine to the cemetery so she and Lisa could ride together. Linda got into the limo with Laura and Mel wondered what they talked about. She wished Laura would give Linda a piece of her mind, but knew her grandmother wouldn't. She liked to keep the peace.

The internment was over within minutes. Laura asked Mel if she and Lisa were coming back to the house, and Mel looked at Linda, who was standing by the limo.

"She's upset," Laura said. "She said you two had words."

"I'm sorry, Grandma, but she gets to me."

"I know. But she is trying."

Mel almost said something hateful about Linda, but stopped herself. Grandma had just buried her mother, a woman she loved.

"I know. We'll come to the apartment."

"See you there."

The same people who went to see Grace off also came to the apartment. Mel and Lisa ate some food, then retreated to Laura's bedroom. Mel lay down and Lisa sat on the edge of the bed.

"I feel bad about this morning," Mel said.

"Why?"

"Because I could have kept my mouth shut. It just felt so good to tell her off."

"Do you want to apologize?"

"Never. I just wish I'd left things alone. She's not gonna grow a conscience just because I yelled at her."

Lisa laughed. "Nope. Probably not."

"Do you ever get mad at your father?"

"Why? Because he leaves me alone so much?"

"Yeah."

"Sometimes I want to yell at him, but he does show up for things like my graduation, so I give him a pass. He has really tried since my mom…Besides, I really don't mind being alone all that much. I did like having you and Sandy at the condo, but it wasn't so bad when you left."

"I thought you were having a pizza and watching a sad movie."

"I did. But then I sat on the porch and listened to the waves. It was nice."

"Do you think you'd like to live down there?"

Lisa lay down, put her head on Mel's legs, and looked at the ceiling.

"I don't know. I like the changing seasons. I don't know if I could live in a place that was warm most of the time."

"I could," Mel said.

"Are you thinking about moving down there?"

"You said I could work anywhere."

Lisa turned and propped herself up on her arm. She looked at Mel. "Did he come to the airport?"

Mel smiled. "Yeah. He kissed me, too."

Lisa smacked Mel's leg. "You didn't tell me."

"It didn't come up."

"So, this is why you're thinking of moving down there."

"It's not the only reason. I thought about what you said, about asking Grandma to come with me."

"Do you think she would?"

"I haven't said anything yet. I'm waiting to see how I feel after the first blizzard."

"Hey, what are they doing about Audrey?"

"She's gonna be cremated and sent up here."

"That's cold."

"It's the easiest way to handle it. Grandma can't afford another funeral."

"Didn't your nana have any money?"

"Not really," Mel said.

"Oh."

"Grandma sold her house before moving in here. Nana had done the same thing years ago and moved into another apartment. I think that money is gone. Grandma could get another place down there, but I think it might be hard for her to get another job."

"I hope she wants to go. Would you go alone?"

Now Mel looked at the ceiling. "I think I would. I can always fly back and forth to see her."

"I could visit, too. We have that time share."

"And I would like to see where this thing with Conner is going."

"I can see you like him, but do you like him?"

Mel smiled. "I do."

"What else happened at the airport?" Lisa asked.

"He said he would come visit in June."

"He did! That's something. Why didn't you tell me?"

"I don't know. I guess there wasn't time."

"Do you think he will?"

"I think he will."

There was a knock on the door.

"Come in," Mel said.

It was Linda. She peeked inside.

"Why don't I see if your grandma needs some help?" Lisa said. She got up and walked past Linda. Linda closed the door.

"Look, I know you have a lot of reasons to hate me, but you don't know what my life has been like. You can't judge me. I'm sorry I haven't always been there for you, but that doesn't mean I don't care."

"What do you want, Linda?"

"For one thing, I want you to call me mom. For another, I want you to…give me a chance."

Mel looked at her. She looked pathetic. Something was wrong. Linda was hurting.

Mel scootched to the edge of the bed and put her feet on the floor. "What's going on, Mom?"

Linda's eyes were downcast. "I went to the doctor. I have…cancer."

"Really, Mom, cancer?"

"I'm not joking. I really do have cancer."

"Have you told Grandma?"

Linda sat on the bed next to Mel. "No. She has enough going on right now. She told me about Audrey. Thank you for helping her with that."

"It was pretty awful. What kind of cancer?"

"Breast. The doctor says if I have a mastectomy, I should be fine. I can even have it reconstructed."

"Then it's not that bad."

"You don't think losing my breast is bad?"

"But you'll have a new one. You'll be alive."

Linda looked into Mel's eyes. She was hoping to see some compassion in her daughter's eyes, but there was none.

"How can you be so cold?" Linda asked. "Even if I weren't your mother, wouldn't you at least feel something as a woman?"

"I do feel something. But I know that with a mastectomy, you should be fine. Especially if they caught it early."

"But it's my breast!" Linda cried.

"It's tissue. Easily replaced tissue. Come on, mom, it's not like you're entering a hospice."

"My God, I don't even know you."

"No, you don't. That's what I was trying to tell you before. You don't know me, but you expect me to act like a daughter to you."

Mel got up and went to the window. Snowflakes were falling past the window. She saw a couple of mourners walking across the parking lot. "Things must be breaking up down there."

"Will you come out when I have the surgery?" Linda asked.

"I have to work. I've taken all the time I can this year."

"I need you."

"I'm sorry. I can't do it."

"I'll have to ask my mother," Linda said.

"She's been out of work a while. She could have used your help when she was in the accident. I don't think she can take any more time off either."

"I'll ask her anyway. She cares about me."

"Yes, she does," Mel said. She turned around and looked at Linda. "And she knows you don't give a damn about anyone but yourself."

"I'm sick," Linda said. Tears rolled down her cheeks.

"But you'll get better."

Linda hadn't expected such a cold reception. The little girl who could be so easily manipulated had turned into an ice queen. Linda didn't know what to do. She had expected Mel to drop everything and come to her aid, but the girl wasn't even concerned about Linda's cancer. What kind of person was she?

Linda got up and left the room. She slammed the bedroom door hard. Mel turned back to the window. She put her hands on the window frame to hold herself up. She was upset and had held it in.

Now she started to cry. The conflicted emotions running through her were wearing her down. She wanted to hate her mother, yet despite everything Linda had done in the course of twenty years, Mel felt compassion for her. But her pride had kept her from showing it.

After everyone left, Mel left the bedroom. She found Laura sitting in the dining room and sat with her.

"Your mother has cancer," she said.

"I know. She told me."

"She wants me to come out there and be with her."

"What about your job?"

"I told her I'd have to think about it."

"I told her I couldn't come."

Laura reached across the table and took Mel's hand. "Thank you for taking the time off for Audrey. I'll go."

"Again, what about your job?"

"I'll get another job."

"I didn't think it was that easy."

Laura sighed. "I know you don't care for her, but she is my daughter. I care about her. She's frightened and she doesn't want to be alone."

"She should have thought of that twenty years ago."

Laura narrowed her eyes. "Mel, this isn't like you. Do you hate your mother?"

"No, I don't hate her. I'm just so mad I could hit her."

"I guess you have a right to be mad. But please, for my sake, let it go. She needs positive thoughts right now."

Mel felt pain in her neck. She had been holding herself so tightly that the muscles in her neck were cramping.

"I will. For you."

Chapter Twenty-Seven

MEL CALLED CONNER TO TELL HIM ABOUT GRACE'S funeral and he told her they had a positive ID on Audrey's body.

"I talked to Jason's attorney," he said. "He convinced Jason a plea bargain would be in his best interest and he had to give the details in open court. Audrey died in her sleep. He found her and panicked, cut a hole in the floor, and buried her, hoping no one would find out. That way he could collect her Social Security and stay in the house. Just like we thought."

"What's gonna happen to him?" Mel asked.

"He's going away for ten years. With good and gain time he should be out in seven. He didn't kill anyone, but the government doesn't like people who steal from them."

"He deserves more."

"Yeah, he does. But he will have to pay it back once he gets out."

"What about her home?" Mel asked.

"That's part of the fraud. The park wants it out. No

one wants to live in a house that had a body buried under it."

"But it belonged to Audrey. It must be worth something."

"Not the way it is. It was an old home, Mel. It wasn't worth more than two or three thousand dollars."

"That little? Geez. She really didn't have anything. I guess I should come down and pack up her things."

"I could do it for you."

"But then I wouldn't have to come down," she said.

"That's true," he said.

"I'll see what flights are available and get back to you. You could start collecting boxes for me."

"I can do that. I'm glad you're coming down."

"I am too."

After Mel hung up the phone, she went to find Laura. Mel had been given a week's bereavement time. If she could get a flight leaving the next day, she'd still have a few days off to spend with Conner. She found Laura in the living room on the sofa, watching her favorite soap opera, and sat next to her.

"They've identified Audrey," Mel said. "I thought I would go down there and pack up her things."

"Oh, that's too much for you. We'll hire someone to do it."

"But I don't mind, Grandma, really I don't."

Laura smiled. "Lisa told me there was a nice-looking policeman helping you while you were down there."

"His name is Conner and he is nice looking."

"He wouldn't have anything to do with your desire to pack up Audrey's house, would he?"

"He might."

Laura put her hand on Mel's. "Okay. But be careful."

"He's very nice. A good guy."

"They all are when you meet them, dear. Just be careful."

"I will."

"Can Lisa go with you?"

"She has to go back to work."

"Well, find out how much the plane ticket costs. I was able to transfer Grace's savings into my account. There wasn't much, but there's enough for the plane ticket."

Mel snuggled next to Laura. "Thanks, Grandma."

"For what?"

"For being so good."

CONNER MET MEL AT THE AIRPORT THAT FRIDAY. HE drove her to his apartment and showed her his bedroom.

"I'll sleep on the couch," he said.

"I'll sleep on the couch. This is your home."

"It's okay. I usually fall asleep on it anyway."

He had boxes stacked in one corner of the room. "We'll take them over there tomorrow. I've got the week off."

She went over to him and put her arms around his waist. "Thank you for helping me."

He bent down and kissed her. "It's no problem. No problem at all."

THE MOBILE HOME WAS IN COMPLETE DISARRAY. THE POLICE had done a search when they arrested Jason and left everything on the floor. Mel sighed when she saw it. Nancy, the park manager, had asked Mel to get any personal items out of the home by the end of January.

The home was being removed and a new one brought in to take its place.

Conner helped her get the place cleaned up. Audrey had kept very little. She had pictures on the shelves, but no photo albums. Her clothes were confined to the closet and her dresser. Jason had occupied the spare room. She boxed up his things and asked Conner to find out what Jason wanted to do with them. He, too, had very little. Mel still didn't understand what had caused her aunt to let him move in.

There was a file box under Audrey's bed. Mel was surprised the cops had missed it, but was glad they had. It contained a will.

In the will, Audrey asked that she be cremated (thank God) and that her ashes be cast into the Gulf of Mexico. Mel liked the idea. She could do it before she left Florida.

It took three days to fill the boxes Conner had collected, and another day to drop them off at Goodwill. In the evenings, she and Conner would have dinner and get to know each other. By the end of the week, Mel was in love. He was a good, stable person, and she adored him. She hoped he felt the same way about her.

ON HER LAST DAY IN FLORIDA, CONNER RENTED A BOAT. Audrey's body had been released to a funeral home and her body cremated. Mel and Conner picked up her urn on their way to the docks and Mel sat it between them in the car.

"I feel like I have to say something," Mel said.

"Most people say something from the Bible."

"I don't think Audrey was religious."

"Then maybe a poem."

"I feel so stupid. I don't know any poems."

"Then don't say anything. I don't think she'll care."

"I don't want my life to end this way," Mel said. "My, God, Conner. She was gone for three months and no one asked why."

He reached over and put his hand on hers. He didn't say anything. As they approached the docks, Mel put her arm around the urn.

"This is it, Audrey."

Mel got out of the car and bent over to get the urn. She held it in her arms and closed the car door with her hip. Conner waited for her.

"Do you want me to carry it?" he asked.

"It's not heavy. I think I have it."

It was a gorgeous day. The wind was light and the sky was true blue. Conner went to the rental stand and signed for the boat. It was a small motor boat big enough for two.

He got in first and held out his arms for the urn. She gave it to him, he put it down, then he gave her his hand so she could get in. Conner sat near the motor and started it while she kept her hands around the urn. She just kept thinking how unfair it all seemed. Her aunt had been ninety. If Mel had never been born, Audrey would have had no one to fulfill her wishes.

"Is this far enough?" Conner asked.

Mel looked toward the docks. "It looks that way."

He cut the motor and they sat. The quiet was unsettling. Mel took the lid off the urn.

"I guess I should say goodbye. Maybe you already found Grace. Tell her I said hi. I only met you once and you smelled nice. You had soft cheeks. Goodbye, Aunt Audrey."

Mel put the urn over the side and turned it upside

down. The wind carried the small particles of ash while the fragments of bone lay on the water, then disappeared.

"What do I do with this?" Mel asked, holding the urn aloft.

"Do you want to keep it?" Conner asked.

"For what?"

"A keepsake?"

Mel looked at the cylindrical, brushed metal container. "I guess I could put flowers in it."

"That sounds good."

"I guess I'll keep it."

"Are you ready to go?"

"Yeah. She's gone."

Conner put the motor on and steered the boat toward the dock. Mel looked to the spot where she had released the ashes and smiled. She had done something good. If karma was to be trusted, someday, someone would do it for her.

Afterword

The story Where's Audrey? is fictional. It is, however, based on an incident that occurred in a Largo, Florida mobile home park in 2007.

What She Deserved

BY A.L. JAMBOR

Prologue

Charlotte Johnson was a true innocent. She had grown up in an orphanage among smaller children and had never been given any instruction on the womanly arts. She had no idea how a woman got pregnant, had no knowledge of birth control, and the only time she'd felt a tingle was when Gary Cooper kissed Sigrid Gurie in The Adventures of Marco Polo.

That kiss was her awakening, but she'd never felt that way toward Arthur Johnson, a boy she'd grown up with at the orphanage who had asked her to marry him so he could secure a job. The Gable Railroad Company favored married men, and they were both going to turn eighteen soon. The clock was ticking and Charlotte, who had no skills and had been told all her life that she was plain and simple, was afraid she might not be able to take care of herself, so she agreed to a marriage in name only.

The job came with a home on the beach in Cape Alden, New Jersey. It was a sparsely furnished one-bedroom Victorian cottage with an indoor toilet, but no bathtub. The kitchen had running water, and if they wanted a bath, they would have to fill an old brass tub from the kitchen faucet.

There was little money for food let alone clothes or toiletries, and Artie, who had envisioned a more prosperous lifestyle, would often sulk and hang out at Morton's Inn, a local bar and restaurant owned by Carl Morton.

Artie met a man named Jack Womack, a sailor who had left his home in England at the age of fourteen. He'd sailed the world, but when he landed in New York in 1930, he had saved enough to buy his own boat and bootlegged whiskey from Canada to Atlantic City. Jack made a fortune, and he didn't mind buying a round for the patrons of the inn. He also felt sorry for poor Artie, married to a woman he didn't love, a woman he found boring and predictable, that is, until Jack met her. Then he felt sorry for Charlotte.

Jack felt a kinship with the tall, awkward girl who lived on the beach and rarely left it to walk into town. Charlotte's shyness endeared her to him, but he never thought of her as anything more than a friend, and she found herself looking forward to his nocturnal visits. He would bring Artie home from Morton's and put him on the sofa, then he and Charlotte would sit on the porch and he would tell her stories of his adventures on the high seas. Jack was a gifted storyteller, and Charlotte, who was starved for attention, would hang on his every word. Her eyes would glisten in the moonlight and Jack's heart would ache for her. She didn't deserve this life, but she was making the most of it.

Every day, as Charlotte waited for Artie to come home, sadness would envelop her. She was married, and divorce was not an option if Artie wanted to keep his job. She didn't know that a lack of physical affection would mean so much to her. Jack was a friend, but he had made it clear that he would never be anything more. He cared about Charlotte, and he knew he was a rambler. Charlotte was ripe for the picking, so when Joe Jackson, the lighthouse keeper flirted with her, she would blush and smile, but she didn't really want Joe. She wanted Gary Cooper.

The day Artie died was the worst day of Charlotte's life. Jack and the sheriff had come to the cottage with the news, and at first, Charlotte didn't believe them. After they assured her he had indeed died, she nodded and thanked the sheriff, but she didn't cry. After the sheriff left, she wept into Jack Womack's shoulder.

Charlotte didn't learn the details of Artie's death until the next day when Jack told her that Artie, who hadn't been with the railroad long, had been sent out to switch the trains, a job that required training. Artie, whose pride prevented him from admitting he'd only watched the tracks being switched, walked down the tracks determined to show them he could do anything. Somehow, he'd been pulled under the passing trains, and his body was cut in half.

The horrific nature of his death caused the Gable Railroad Company to offer Charlotte free use of the cottage indefinitely, and they also offered a small stipend to help her in her time of need. Any resulting litigation would have cost them far more, and they used Mrs. Johnson's youth and ignorance of the law to their advantage. Jack was livid when he heard, but Charlotte refused to cause the railroad any trouble, and accepted their offer with gratitude.

When it was warm, Charlotte would watch Joe Jackson's children, Birdie, 6, Myrna, 4, and Kerry, 3, play on the beach. She longed to join them, to run into the ocean as the waves washed the shore, or make sandcastles. She was lonely, and now that she was single, the ladies in town rebuffed her attempts at conversation.

Joan Jackson, Joe's wife, was particularly hard on Charlotte, for Joan knew her husband had a wandering eye, and the young widow lived a mere half-mile from their door. Joan's hatred toward her kept Charlotte from engaging the girls in conversation as they ran past her porch.

Charlotte had even tried joining the small church in town, hoping to show that she was a good person, but her reputation, fueled by Joe's tales of a relationship with Charlotte and his wife's jealousy, had grown too big for her to contain, and she soon stopped attending services.

When Jack was in town, he would visit, and the gossip mill would rumble with stories of his leaving her cottage in the morning. Jack, mindful of what they were saying, would always leave at ten and stop at Morton's before going up to one of Morton's rooms. Carl Morton kept it for him. The family occupied the other rooms, and Carl's wife, Celia, would always smile when she met Jack in the hallway on her way to the bathroom. She thought he looked like Clark Gable.

Jack would also give Charlotte money from time to time. He bought her some new clothes, and would take her to Atlantic City. He bought her food and she would cook, delighted to have a friend, but she was getting older. She wanted to start taking care of herself.

One day, she saw a "Help Wanted" sign in the window of the ice company. A glimmer of hope rose inside her as she went inside and smiled at the secretary sitting behind the desk. It was her job Charlotte would be applying for. The woman was getting married and would no longer need a job, but she wanted her replacement to a good person. She recognized

Charlotte as that floozy who lived near the ocean. She looked at Charlotte's dress, the one she'd been married in two years before, and noted the worn edges on the sleeves and the collar. The woman looked down her nose at Charlotte and smiled.

"The position has been filled."

Charlotte's own smile faded as she thanked the woman for telling her. While she might be innocent in many ways, Charlotte wasn't stupid, and she knew she'd been rejected because of the things they said about her in town. She almost went into Morton's Inn to ask for a glass of whiskey, but she didn't have the nerve to go there alone. Instead, she stood between the ice company and the store next to it and sobbed.

Winter 1940

The freezing rain had pummeled the cottage for hours, and Charlotte looked at the empty cupboard above her sink in dismay. She was hungry. She had three dollars in her purse to last another two weeks, money left over from Jack, and despite the rain, she decided to put on her slicker and walk to town.

She ran her hand over the baby bump and felt sad. She hadn't told him yet, and was afraid someone would find out. The ladies in town would send her out of town on a rail.

Her clothes were still loose enough to hide her condition, and with a slicker on, no one would notice she had "put on a little weight." She walked down the walkway and felt the rain hitting her legs. The temperatures had dropped, turning the rain to snow, and she tried not to stumble as she walked to the road.

Charlotte was walking past the lighthouse on the other

side of the road when she felt someone grab her arm and whirl her around.

"You stay away from my family, you whore."

Joan smacked Charlotte's face so hard that she fell backward onto the dirt. Joan spit on her and left her on the muddy, cold ground. Her tears were flowing freely now, and they grew worse as Charlotte tried to get back on her feet.

The mud was slippery, and it covered her legs and skirt. She managed to right herself and headed back to the cottage, gulping for breath as her sobs intensified. She felt impotent, like a non-person who had no right to be alive. Charlotte was a whore; the whole town knew it, and any who doubted it would soon have their doubts confirmed as the child inside her grew.

She took her slicker off on the porch, along with her shoes and her dress. She shivered in the cold, but she didn't want to drag mud into the house. After she washed the mud off herself, she could change and wash the mud off her clothes.

She went inside and dragged the brass tub out from underneath the sink so she could bathe. The railroad had promised to install a shower, but once Artie died, there was little reason for them to invest in the cottage. Guilt had allowed her to stay there, and they felt that was enough.

She filled the old brass tub with a bucket and water from the kitchen sink, but the pipe from the hot water heater had frozen and burst. The water was clean but cold and she shivered as she washed her legs. After drying off and getting dressed, she retrieved her clothes and washed them, too.

Firewood was stacked on the porch. She'd forgotten to bring it in so it could dry, so after she brought in a couple of logs, she tried to light it, but the fire wouldn't take. She was shivering so hard she couldn't stop, and she began to sob again. Why was she such a mess? Why couldn't she remember something as important as firewood?

Because you're stupid, Charlotte.

Artie had said it all the time. You're stupid. She'd heard it in school, too, and if so many people believed it, it must be true. That's why she was in such a mess now. Jack would have been so disappointed in her. He'd get mad whenever she called herself a dummy.

"You're not dumb," he'd say. "You just look at life differently."

A knock on the door surprised her and she wiped her face. She walked across the room, looked out the window, and then she remembered what Joan had said. She opened the door and he saw her red eyes.

"Go," she said.

"Birdie told me what she did," he said.

"Please go."

"Please let me in."

She felt ashamed and bruised and hurt. Joan's admonition had been hard to take, and she didn't want to be confronted by her again. Besides, what had started off as something sweet and wonderful had turned into something she feared. He often came to her with good intentions only to become angry over something she said or did that annoyed him.

"Please go home before she sees."

"I'm not letting you go," he said.

"I can't fight her. You have to stay away."

"I don't care what she wants. I want you."

As he always did, he overwhelmed her with his smooth words, his promises, and his pseudo love. She was so hungry for human affection that she embraced it, even though she knew it would soon turn ugly. He took her arm and they went inside.

She went to the tub to remove her clothes and as she bent over, he came up behind her and put his hands on her waist.

"We've never tried it this way," he said. She swallowed hard so she wouldn't gag.

"I have to hang these clothes."

But he was lifting her skirt, and rubbing her thighs, and then he reached around and felt her stomach. His hands stopped and he backed away.

She stood up and moved away from the tub.

"Is that a baby?" he asked.

"I think so," she said softly.

He didn't say anything but began pacing the floor.

"It's my baby."

"Yes."

"Why didn't you tell me?"

"I wasn't sure, but it's getting bigger."

He stopped pacing and stared at her.

"I'm gonna take care of you."

She was shocked by his reaction. She thought he would be upset, that he would rant about how she'd ruined his life, but he looked happy. She shivered and he saw it.

"Let's sit down and I'll warm you up," he said.

She knew what that meant, that he would want to make love, and though she enjoyed their lovemaking, she wasn't in the mood for it after her encounter with Joan. He came and took her hand and led her to the sofa. He put his arm around her shoulder and began kissing her neck and cupping her breast, but when she didn't respond as he expected, he squeezed her breast hard.

"What's wrong?" he said.

"Nothing."

He tried to arouse her again, and felt her stiffen. Anger flared, and his hand went to her cheek as if it was out of his control, and the sharp pang of regret that always followed didn't soothe her nerves.

"Why do you make me do this?" he asked. He held himself and exhaled. "I'm sorry."

He got up and began pacing the floor. Charlotte drew her legs up and wrapped her arms around them. She waited for the next assault, the one that would send her to the floor, and then the apologies, and promises that it would never happen again.

She thought of her suitcase in the bedroom. She had pawned her wedding ring months ago, so she had nothing, no money or anything of value to sell, but she had to get away. She couldn't risk him hurting the baby, or worse, killing her.

As he paced the floor telling her how much he loved her, she held her legs tighter. Whatever it took, she would find a way to get out of this town, and away from the man she loved.

Marigold Burnside
Day 3

"I don't want anything to happen to you."

It was a male voice. She couldn't see his face, but he made her feel safe. Lights coming toward her, squealing brakes, a scream – who was screaming ? – and crunching metal.

She opened her eyes, looked at a mass of blurry dots, and then closed her eyes again.

The sound of a machine woke her, but only for a moment, and then she closed her eyes again.

The plastic tube inserted in her throat was irritating, and she lifted her hand to pull it out.

"You're awake!" The cheery female voice sounded too loud. "Oh, you mustn't do that. Dr. Fletcher will be in shortly to remove it."

Mari blinked. The dots overhead were coming into focus now, and she was able to identify the sound of the ventilator. The woman came to her side so Mari could see her face. The woman smiled.

"Your color is good." The woman wore a hat. "Oh, it's good to see you with your eyes open!"

Mari looked to her right and saw a window. The sky was a mass of gray clouds. She couldn't tell what time it was, but now she was aware of pain in her shoulder, pelvis, and legs. She moaned, and the woman shook her head.

"Mustn't try to talk, dear. Just breathe normally."

Mari closed her eyes.

Someone was touching her wrist. Mari opened her eyes and saw a woman wearing scrubs. Her soft brown eyes glanced at Mari's and she smiled.

"Welcome back," she said.

Mari looked at her badge but couldn't see her name. She listened to Mari's heart and then went to a laptop on a stand to notate Mari's file.

"You're lungs sound good," she said. "I think the doctor is going to take out your tube today."

Mari tried to smile, but it looked more like a grimace and the woman smiled.

"Yeah, that makes you happy, doesn't it?"

Mari nodded and closed her eyes.

"Must get your strength up."

The cheerful woman in the hat was back.

"Dr. Fletcher is on his way. He'll be here any minute now."

Mari closed her eyes.

"Marigold." It was a man's voice. Mari opened her eyes. A man in scrubs smiled at her. "We're going to take the tube out."

Mari assumed this was Dr. Fletcher. Several young people were assisting him and they removed the tape keeping the tube in place.

"Are you ready?" the doctor asked. Mari nodded. "One, two, three..."

He pulled it out and Mari choked. A young woman standing next to her held her head up and another held a kidney-shaped plastic dish underneath her chin. When they were sure she wouldn't vomit, they let her go. She lay back on her pillow and breathed.

"Are you in any pain?" the doctor asked.

"Yes." Mari's voice was hoarse. The young woman grabbed her drinking cup and held it in front of her mouth. Mari took a sip.

"I'll leave an order for medication," he said. "You're going to be tired. Don't fight it. You need to rest." He noted something in the laptop. "I'll be in tomorrow morning. Do you have any questions?"

"Where am I?" she mouthed.

"Oceanville General Hospital. You were in an accident."

Screeching tires. Crunching metal. Black ice. Mari closed her eyes against the memory.

Mari
Day 5

"How was your night?" Mari's heart jumped. It was the woman in the hat. "Did you evacuate your bowels?"

"Not yet."

"Well, then, we might have to help it along."

Her shit had become a frequent topic of conversation since she'd woken up. She knew what "help it along" meant and wished she'd said, "Yes, I passed a big one this morning," but it was too late now.

Mari looked at the hat and thought it looked like the ones nurses wore years ago. The woman held a chart and a pen, and she wore glasses. Her uniform was white, and when she walked away, Mari noted that she wore white stockings and shoes. The other nurses wore scrubs, so the woman's daily appearance was a mystery. She was also the only one using a chart and pen to take notes.

"I keep forgetting to ask you your name," Mari said.

The woman looked over the rim of her glasses at Mari. "I'm Nurse Cabot. Do you remember what happened to you?"

"I was in an accident."

"Good girl." The nurse noted the chart. "Do you know what day it is?"

"No."

"Do you know what month it is?"

"No."

Mari's voice was still raspy, and her throat hurt. The nurse's pitiful look pissed her off. Mari knew what she was thinking – poor Marigold. Her mind is mush.

Mari closed her eyes and swallowed.

"I need some water."

She waited for the nurse to say something, and when she didn't, Mari opened her eyes and saw that the nurse was gone. She searched for the remote and pushed the buttons until it started raising her head. The dizzy, swimming sensation she felt was awful, so she took her thumb off the button and went back down. She closed her eyes again, but that made it worse. She felt cold. She felt sad, or was it depression? She could never tell the difference.

"'Morning, Miss Burnside."

The nurse in scrubs was back. The name on her badge read "Cassandra Torrance, R.N." "I'm Cassie. You're looking all chipper this morning."

"I'm sure," Mari said.

The nurse smiled. "Is your head still swimming?" Mari nodded. "It might get better if you sit up."

"I tried."

"And what happened?"

"It got worse."

Cassie typed some notes into Mari's digital chart, and then came to the side of the bed and put a thermometer in Mari's mouth before she took her pulse and blood pressure.

"Your temp is normal and your blood pressure is low."

Cassie entered the numbers into the computer. She glanced at Mari, and her eyes radiated sympathy. Mari liked her, even when she pushed the button on her bed remote and raised Mari's head. The dizziness made her stomach churn.

"I've gotta go down," Mari said.

"Let's just do this for a minute."

Mari swallowed hard and fought the urge to hit Cassie.

"Please let me down."

"A few more seconds."

Her head began to clear and her eyes focused. She could see out the window now, and saw that the cars in the parking lot were covered in snow. Her breathing settled, but the pain between her eyes grew worse.

"My head hurts."

"Do you remember what happened to you?" Cassie asked.

"I already told that other nurse."

Cassie looked at her strangely. "What did you tell her?"

"That I was in an accident."

"That's right, and you hit your head pretty hard. You were in a coma for two days." Cassie picked up Mari's wrist. "See this band? It says 'I can't walk alone.' That means you can't get out of bed by yourself, so don't try going to the bathroom yet. Call us and we'll bring you a bedpan."

"Oh, God," Mari said.

"It's not so bad. You'll have people waiting on you hand and foot."

"I hurt all over."

"I brought your pain medication."

Cassie handed her a small paper cup and filled Mari's Styrofoam cup with water. After Mari swallowed the pills, Cassie made notes in the computer.

"That other nurse didn't use the computer," Mari said.

Cassie didn't look up as she typed. When she'd finished her entries, she came over and put her hand on Mari's forehead.

"Didn't you take my temperature?"

"Yes, but I'm double checking."

"Why?"

Cassie looked at her and brushed Mari's hair away from her eyes.

"Because I'm your nurse for the day. I'm the only one who's been in here this morning."

Mari
Day 7

Day 7

Mari felt someone standing near her and opened her eyes. It was the woman in the hat, and she was staring at Mari.

"She didn't mean to hurt you," the woman said.

"What?"

The woman faded away as Cassie walked into the room.

"You're awake," Cassie said.

"I just woke up."

"How are you feeling?"

"A little better."

"Tell her to move you." Mari looked toward the window and saw a man in a nightshirt standing at the end of her bed. "You are in my bed, young woman, and I won't stand for it."

Cassie held Mari's wrist and felt her pulse jump. She looked at her patient, and then followed Mari's gaze to the window.

"What was that?" Cassie asked.

"What was what?"

"Your pulse jumped."

"That's weird."

"Mmm huh."

Cassie took her blood pressure and noticed it was higher than the day before. Patients with head injury often experienced anxiety, which sometimes caused them to feel overwhelmed. Mari was still wearing her "I can't walk alone" band, but that wouldn't keep her from getting out of bed to run from something she thought was happening.

"How did you sleep last night?" Cassie asked.

"I woke up a couple of times."

"Could you go right back to sleep?"

Mari shook her head. "My back hurts and this bed is hard."

"I asked you to move her. This is my bed."

Mari glared at the old man, and Cassie looked at the window again. She went to the laptop and noted in the chart that Mari might need a psych evaluation.

"The doctor wants you to sit in the recliner during the day, and the physical therapist is going to visit. They want you to be ready to go to rehab, and I'll bet you want to get out of this hospital, too."

"Get her out now!"

The old man's hands balled into fists and he stomped his foot, causing Mari to giggle.

"It's good to hear you laugh," Cassie said. "Something tickled you."

"Oh, I was just thinking about how much my priorities have changed. Sitting in a recliner is actually considered progress."

Cassie was pulling the sheet off Mari so she could help her out of bed, and Mari stuck her tongue out at the old man.

"Ready?" Cassie asked.

Mari's leg hurt when she moved it toward the edge of the bed, but she kept going. She was more comfortable in the recliner, but she still got dizzy when she stood, so she couldn't get into it alone. She still needed someone to walk with her to the bathroom, and when she was allowed to take a shower, she had to sit on a chair while she bathed.

The stiffness in her joints was getting better, but her broken pelvis was taking its time, and the pain in her hip was still bad. She didn't feel so brittle anymore, just achy and tired.

Her physical injuries had taken precedence over the memory problems she was having, though, and she asked Cassie when someone would come to help her with that.

"You might not see anyone until we get you to rehab."

"But I can't remember the accident."

"You have to give it time, Marigold."

"Mari. Please call me Mari."

"You suffered a traumatic head injury. Your brain is bruised and it might take longer to heal than your arms and legs."

"Will I remember it?"

Cassie raised her eyebrows. "I'm not qualified to answer that, but if you want, I can put in a request for the psychiatrist to see you."

"Please do that."

Cassie changed her note from "might need" to "does need" a visit from the psychiatrist. She finished her notes and smiled at Mari.

"I think breakfast is coming."

She pushed Mari's tray to the recliner and lowered it for her.

"I wrote on your file that you want to see a psychiatrist. Do you have to go before I leave?"

Mari shook her head. "Not yet."

"Okay, then I'll see you later."

The old man got into Mari's bed and pulled imaginary covers over himself.

"Who are you?" she asked.

"That's none of your business."

She watched him fade away and felt a shiver go up her spine. Why was she seeing these apparitions? What part of the brain allowed you to see ghosts? Would this happen forever, or just until her brain healed?

Mari turned on the TV and watched a local station out of Oceanville, New Jersey.

Why am I in Oceanville? she thought.

She flipped through channels until she found the news. She looked at the photo of a mangled car behind the newscaster.

"There are still no charges in the death of hotelier Harry Miller. Mr. Miller was the passenger in a car driven by Marigold Burnside, a reporter for the TV show, Historic Homicides. Ms. Burnside was in Cape Alden to research the unsolved murder of Charlotte Johnson, who died in 1941. The driver of the other car, Philip Curry of Cape Alden, was thought to be driving under the influence, but tests have cleared him of any wrongdoing. Mr. Curry stated that he swerved to avoid a pedestrian, but so far, the police have been unable to confirm this. Mr. Miller's death is blamed in part on the failure of the airbags to deploy. This particular brand of airbags was part of a massive recall issued several months ago."

Marigold Burnside. She was Marigold Burnside. She had been driving the car and a man was killed.

"I don't want anything to happen to you."

Flashes of flames in a fireplace, the taste of red wine, and Christmas lights blinking raced through her mind.

Mari remembered checking into the B&B. She remembered the man behind the desk as she filled out the paperwork. He was nice, and his smile was sweet. She had liked him the moment she saw him. It wasn't like her to fall for someone so fast, but he was different. She trusted him.

Harry Miller. That was his name. He owned the B&B. They'd hit it off right away. He had green eyes...

"...the death of hotelier Harry Miller."

He was kind. He liked cooking for her, and touching her cheek. It had been a long time since she'd met a man who got her, who liked her snarky sense of humor, and made her feel special.

"...the death of hotelier Harry Miller."

"Oh, my God! I killed him."

The woman in the hat appeared. She held a chart and the pen was poised to take notes.

"What do you want?" Mari cried.

"Have you moved your bowels today?"

"Are you kidding? No, I haven't shit yet, okay?"

"No need for profanity, dear."

She jotted something on the chart and faded away when Mari's breakfast arrived. The young woman put the tray on the cart and took the menu for the next day. Mari couldn't remember filling it out. Her short-term memory loss was acute and she worried about doing something awful and forgetting what she'd done. The only thing she did remember was the ghosts that kept appearing out of nowhere.

She felt the tears in her eyes and wondered why she had been crying.

"Damn it."

The news was on. The news. Something on the news had upset her. She wiped the tears away and ate her breakfast. When she was done, emotions rose in her and she began to cry again, sobbing so hard her tears dampened the front of her gown.

An hour later, Cassie came in to take her vitals, and she saw Mari's eyes.

"You okay?" she asked. "You look like you've been crying."

"I have been. I just don't know why." Mari looked at the TV. "Maybe it was something on the TV."

"I should have unplugged that thing." Cassie pushed the button on the remote to turn off the TV.

"Why can't I watch TV?"

Cassie turned the TV back on.

"Did I have a purse or bag?"

"It's in the drawer next to you."

Mari opened the drawer of the small end table next to her bed. She took the bag out and found her wallet. She looked at her driver's license, but she couldn't focus her eyes to read it.

"Please read it for me."

Cassie took the wallet from Mari. "It says you were born on July 16, 1982."

"How old does that make me?"

Cassie did the math in her head. "35. It says you are an organ donor, and you have a New York address."

"What else does it say?"

"Nothing else." Cassie looked at her.

"I have a job. Is my phone in here?"

Mari put her hand in her bag and found her phone.

"Be careful about talking to people," Cassie said. "Sometimes you say some strange things after you hit your head."

Mari held the phone. Pain at the front of her head made her close her eyes. She'd been given Oxycodone, but after seven days, they stopped and gave her Ibuprofen. It worked, but not as well. She laid her head back and closed her eyes.

"My head hurts."

"It's almost time for your meds."

Cassie helped her to the bathroom. Mari looked at her face in the mirror and sighed.

"I look like death warmed over," she said.

"You look better than you did last week," Cassie said. "Do you want to take a shower?"

"Maybe later. I'm so tired."

Cassie got her back into the recliner and left her with the promise of a shower later that afternoon. The drone of the TV voices made her drowsy.

"Mari."

It was her mother's voice.

"Mom."

"Hi, Honey. It's time to get up. You can't miss the bus today."

Mari opened her eyes. Cassie was standing in front of her with a small cup in her hand.

"It's time for your meds."

Mari blinked a few times, looked out the window, and then at Cassie.

"Was I asleep?"

"Sure looked that way."

Mari took the cup with her meds from Cassie, who then handed her a cup of water.

"I saw my mom," Mari said.

"Oh?"

"She was telling me I couldn't miss the bus."

"I do that with my son all the time."

"My mom died last year." Tears appeared in the corners of her eyes. "She had cancer."

Mari wiped the tears away.

"So you've had a really bad year," Cassie said.

Cassie held Mari's hand while her patient sobbed.

She'd been trying to find someone from Mari's family to come and see her, but when Cassie talked to Mari's roommate in New York City, he'd told her that Mari didn't have any family. She was all alone in the world.

Cassie tried to maintain a professional distance from her patients because at the end of the day, you had to go home, and the pain of seeing someone you truly cared about suffering would break your heart, but this patient was getting to her. She liked Mari, and wanted to take her pain away. Cassie had thought about being reassigned because her judgment could be affected by her feelings, but losing someone she'd grown used to might make Mari more anxious, so she stayed.

Cassie owned a home in Cape Alden she shared with her six-year-old son, Joey. The garage in the back of the house had an apartment that Cassie had fixed up to rent. As she held Mari's hand, she thought about that apartment. Mari had suffered a severe head trauma. The doctors in the ER thought she would die, but she was a fighter. She'd survived and they were all thrilled when she woke up, but Cassie knew it would take a long time for her to recover. Even then, she might never be the same person again. What would she do if she couldn't work?

Mari had drifted off. She looked peaceful, so Cassie pulled her hand from Mari's and left the room. She had already decided that if Mari needed it, she could have the apartment over Cassie's garage.

Click here to buy or borrow *What She Deserved* with Kindle Unlimited.

About the Author

A.L. Jambor began writing in 2010. Inspired by a photo of her granddaughter, she sat at her computer and wrote the harrowing story of a pharmaceutical nightmare called But the Children Survived. The book was a hit, and she went on to write more books and novellas, including the popular Divine Detective Agency.

In 2013, she began a time travel series called The Secret of Truelock Manor. The third book in the series, Mercy in the Moonlight, while a good story, wasn't the tale Ms. Jambor wanted to tell. She revisited the series, choosing to combine the three books, and that book became Their Best Dreams.

Ms. Jambor lives with her husband in Florida. They share their home with a dog named Trixie, the inspiration for "Baby Girl" in But the Children Survived, and the pudgy terrier, Libby the Psychic Dog. A cat named Sammy rounds out their little family. She welcomes communication with her fans.

Visit ALJambor.com for information and updates.

Novels

But the Children Survived

Dangerous Stranger

Their Best Dreams

Where's Audrey?

A Tender Heart

Don't Look Back

What She Deserved

A Lethal Legacy

Novellas

The Room in Grandma's House

Kevin Chandler and The Case of the Missing Dogs

The House on the Shore

The Christmas Cottage

A Christmas Mystery

Divine Detective Agency Mystery Shorts:

The Body in the Bungalow

The Devious Dame

The Kid at the Candy Counter

Libby the Psychic Dog in:

Libby the Psychic Dog

Mystery in the Mansion

Quandary on the Quay

The Nefarious Neighbor

The Cat's Confession